Charles Aldrich

Green Ivy Publishing
1 Lincoln Centre
18W140 Butterfield Road
Suite 1500
Oakbrook Terrace IL 60181-4843
www.greenivybooks.com

ISBN: 978-1-942901-88-4

❈
I MEET Abbrelle

INTRODUCTION

This is the story of how I met my wife, Abbrelle, and our adventures on her home world of Home Pride. Home Pride is a planet in the Bright Star planetary system. The system has two suns that orbit the planet, each on opposite sides of the planet. One of the suns orbits over the Northern Hemisphere and the other above the Southern. The average temperature is one hundred five degrees and the humidity is 70 percent.

I am the author of the best-selling fiction series Jim Star–Space Ranger, as well as other best-selling books.

I live in the small town of Beaman in southern California, a few miles inland from the ocean and several miles from mountains.

I am six foot three, one hundred ninety pounds, well-built, with light brown hair.

I MEET Abbrelle

CHAPTER 1

As I stumbled across the burning sands, the stars began to fade as the morning sun slowly crept over the horizon, brightening up the barren landscape.

I looked down the slope at the little pool of life-giving water, as it lies there in the shade of the trees. There was no breeze and the tall grass was not moving even as much as a single leaf.

I slowly started to make my way down to the pool of water. As I crawled, I tried to stay hidden and not move the grass—the grass with razor sharp blades.

I crawled closer to the water and scared a rabbit-like creature—the sight of which reminded me how hungry I was.

My right shoulder was starting to ache from the wound I had received earlier. Crawling forward, trying to reach the pooling water through the thick and prickly vegetation, and finally sliding up to the edge of the pool, I began to take slow, shallow drinks of the life-giving water. As I lay by the pool, the cool water soothing my parched throat, I heard a noise off to my left. Rolling under a low bush, I tried to be quiet and stay out of sight.

I saw a Craig emerge out of the tall undergrowth, looking around, trying to locate me. I knew he was looking for me because he was the creature who had shot me the day before.

A Craig is a manlike creature with a reptilian face, hands, feet, and a tail. It walks on two legs like a man but has a large tail for extra balance when it to hit you with. The Craig had invaded this far off world of Ice Star Five one Cycle ago.

Ice Star five orbits the sun of Ice Star. Ice Star was named by the exploration team that discovered the sun and the five orbiting planets. They named it Ice Star because of the ice-like, shimmering color and its extreme heat.

I looked down at the words that I had written on the page, ripping it out of my typewriter, and throwing the crumpled paper in the wastebasket— now overflowing with discarded paper from all of my attempts to start this new book in the Jim Star - Space Ranger series. The series of books I was writing.

I'm Steven Stevenson, author of the space series: Jim Star– Space Ranger. *Have you read them? The first six have been best sellers.*

I said to myself, "That's too much like what I did to him in Book 6." I looked at the pile of discarded paper growing on the floor, overflowing from the wastebasket.

As I wondered what I could do that would hold the readers' attention, my own attention was broken when the front doorbell started ringing. Actually it rang continually like someone was leaning on the button.

I walked to the door and looked through the side window to see if I could identify who was so being so rude as to ring the bell that way. At the door was the silhouette of what looked like a small child— standing with her finger pressed on the doorbell.

I opened the door, getting ready to yell at her for disturbing me. When she turned around to look at me, my mouth dropped open in surprise. Expecting a small child, it turned out to be a petite young woman—barely five tall. She was about eighteen or nineteen years old with shoulder-length blond hair. She was wearing a knee-length black, backless dress and looked as if she had just come from a classy party.

She stood with her body turned sideways, looking back toward the street, still pressing on the doorbell. She looked as if she excepted to be attacked by someone at any moment.

"You can stop holding the button in now," I said looking at her. "I'm here. What do you want?" I asked . . . somewhat irritated.

"Can I come in . . . please?" she asked, looking at me, with her big doe eyes.

"I suppose if you have to," I answered irritably, stepping back out of the doorway. "What do you want?"

She stayed in the doorway. "I want to find Jim Star." She looked up at me with those big eyes and long lashes.

"He's not here. You know he is just a character in my books. Don't you?"

"He's not . . . He is? You mean you penned those 'Tell Abouts' for all of his adventures?" She looked at me with a forlorn look. "But . . . . he has to be more than just a character in a book. I need his help." She wailed. "If he cannot help us, we're doomed. We are all doomed."

Charles Aldrich

"I'll help you if I can." What else could I say?

She gave me another forlorn look. "I do not know. We had planned on Jim Star helping us. It's something he seems to do so well."

"Well, tell me what your problem is and I will see if I can help," I replied . . . now clearly baffled.

"Well I am from a planet outside of this solar system. We call our planet Home Pride. We were returning there when we experienced some trouble with our ship. We had explored a small planet where we discovered a satellite that had crashed on it. In the satellite we found a series of books about Jim Star and thought he could help us."

"But then how did you get here?" I asked. "And why did they send you?"

"Well, how we got here . . ." she started saying, somewhat puzzled. "Aaahh . . . well, we had enough power left in our ship to either send me here and get Jim Star or to try to get home— which we can't do at this time for reasons I cannot say now. We thought he would help a poor, defenseless girl," she said, looking up at me again with her big, pleading doe eyes.

"You know that sound a little far-fetched. Don't you?" I replied as I looked down at her.

"It does?" She looked clearly confused.

"Yes . . . Are you playing a joke on me?" I asked, looking into her upturned face.

"It's not a joke," she said. "We are from Bright Star. We were looking to find some help, to help us fight against the MAMI and our ship broke down. We think they are trying to overthrow our government. We are stranded here until we can get our ship repaired and were hoping that he could help us. One of the engines quit working."

"What is MAMI?" I asked.

"The Movement Against Moral Indecency," she quietly replied.

I didn't inquire further about MAMI. The subject seemed to bother her. "How did you know about Jim Star?"

"Well," she said, looking coyly. "We can read minds sometimes and . . . do other things with our minds too. You were thinking so hard about Jim Star that I picked up on your thoughts clear out in the path. I thought maybe he could help us."

"Why did you hold the doorbell in for so long?"

"Your mind said to push the button in to let you know I was here. It never said to stop.

"Why do you think Jim Star can help you?" I asked, still looking at her.

"Because Jim Star does so much—I thought you would know how to find him. And we could get the part we need to fix our ship."

"He is just a fictional character in the books I write," I repeated.

"Why do you want me to take this . . . *dress* . . . off?" she asked suddenly, lifting her hands up to unhook the straps of the dress.

"Stop!" I exclaimed and grabbed her hands. "What are you doing?"

"Well, you were thinking so hard about what I looked like without this . . . *dress* . . . that I thought I would show you." She still had her hands on the straps.

"We are not use to wearing all of these coverings. We never wear anything above our hips on the ship or on our home planet" She said as I held her wrists against her neck.

"Well, be that as it may. Here we keep our bodies covered."

"Even when you sleep?" she asked

"Yes some people do." I replied

"Well I saw some . . . *people* . . . by the water and they did not have all these . . . *clothes* . . . on. Especially on top."

"That's different. Men don't wear tops when they swim."

"Why do men not have tops on when the swim but women do?"

"That's a good question." I said looking at her. "How long have you been here?" I was starting to doubt her story again. "Maybe I can explain it to you some other time. Why should I believe you are from outer space anyway?"

She then got a dreamy look on her face. At the same time I started to see a vision in my mind of half dressed people in what could be a spacecraft going about different duties—such as preparing food, operating and servicing the ship.

"That's quite trick," I said, still seeing the scene in my head. "How are you doing that?"

"I told you we can read minds sometimes. It's not hard to make some people see what we want them to see. Some of us are pretty good at making them see what we want them to see," she said. "As with this dress."

"So you are telling me that you are controlling my thoughts right now."

"Yes . . . somewhat," she replied.

"What would I have to do to stop you from controlling my thoughts?"

"You answered that yourself in Jim Star's last book."

"I see." I let my mind go blank, trying to close my mind to hers as Jim Star had done in his last book—after being captured by mind-controlling aliens. "Did you get that from my mind to?" I asked, looking at her more sternly.

"Yes, I told you we can read thoughts. Most have learned to control their thoughts . . . somewhat."

It took almost five minutes, but she started to shimmer and her clothes faded away, leaving her standing simply in a pair of very short shorts . . . just like I had seen the others wearing on the ship—shorts and topless.

"You shouldn't be walking around like that," I said, continuing to stare at her bare breasts. "We don't go around dressed like that here." I pulled her in the door before someone could see her standing there topless. "I'll get you something to wear. Why did you come here dressed in that dress anyway?"

"I saw it on a person down the . . . *road* . . . a few roads over, and I had noticed that everyone had different coverings on than I did. So I created this . . . *dress.*"

"You mean streets. Did anyone see you before you created the dress—before you made the dress?" I asked as I rummaged through my clean clothes for something for her to wear.

"I don't think so, but one person may have. He looked at me funny. What is . . . *created?*"

"Create means to make something," I said. "Good!" I said as handed her a T-shirt. "Creating is what you did with that dress."

She looked at the T-shirt. "What do I do with this?" she asked.

"You pull it over your head and cover yourself with it," I said, watching her try to figure out the T-shirt.

"How?" She asked. It was clear from her expression that said she did not understand the mechanics of putting on a T-shirt.

I held it up. "You put your arms through these holes, like this." I demonstrated by putting my own arms in the sleeves. "And your head through this one." Again, I demonstrated by pulling the shirt over my head. "And then you pull it down over the rest of your body."

"Why?" she asked.

"Because women do not walk around with their . . . breasts

exposed," I said.

"What are . . . *breasts?*" she asked.

Those!" I pointed at her chest."

"Oh! But why? We always do," she said. "Is that why the . . . *women* . . . I saw, all had their . . . *breasts* . . . covered?" She touched her chest and looked up at me.

"Yes!" I answered, and pushed the T-shirt to her. She started to put it on.

"It's awfully tight around here," she said, pulling at the neck.

"That's because you have it on backwards. Take your arms out of the sleeves and turn it around."

Instead she took it off and handed it to me. "You turn it around then." Looking frustrated, she held the T-shirt out.

I took it, turned it around and holding it out for her to put it on saying. "Put your arms through here," I said indicating the sleeves. I pulled the shirt over her head and pulled it down below her waist—making a dress as she was so short.

"It's too big!" she said as she pulled the sleeves up.

Ignoring the statement I asked. "Now what seems to be the matter with your ship?"

"It's this thing here," she said, handing me what looked like a starter relay from a car, which she had taken from *somewhere* in her shorts. Her shorts did not look as if they could hide anything—they were so tight. "The engine will not start from the bridge. This," she said, nodding toward the relay, "is supposed to let it start from the bridge."

"If this is all that is wrong with your craft, I think we can get you a new one tomorrow when the auto parts store opens in the morning."

"What is an . . . *auto parts* . . . store?" she asked, looking questioningly at me.

"It's a place we go to get parts to fix our Autos."

"What is an auto?" she asked.

"A device we use for transportation here on Earth."

"What is . . . *Earth?*"

I stared at her and said "This planet, we call it Earth."

"Oh," she said. "We call it Star 5005742, Planet 3."

"You can stay here in the spare bedroom until we go and get the part tomorrow morning."

"What is a . . . *spare bedroom* . . . ?" she asked.

"It is a place to sleep," I said before she could finish asking.

"What is . . . *sleep?*" She asked looking at me questioningly.

"It is how we rest." I answered— exasperated.

"Why can I not sleep with you? I sleep with others on the ship? We all . . . *sleep* . . . in one large room. Quite often two to a rest pad. There are never enough for everyone. It can get noisy if someone is 'talking' too loudly when you are trying to sleep. If it gets too loud, we just start 'talking' to whomever we are resting with. I have 'talked' to many . . . *men.* They all seem to like talking to me and my sister best," she said, again looking at me with an inquiring expression.

"Well we don't here, unless . . ." I abruptly replied, and then turned away.

When we got up the next morning, she looked as if she had slept on the floor all night; her clothes were rumpled and dirty.

"Where did you sleep?" I asked.

"Sleep?"

I rolled my eyes. "Yes, spend the night, you know rest?"

"There," she said, pointing at the floor. That object there was too nice and soft to sleep on."

"But that's what it is for. It is suppose to be soft. It is called a bed. OK—I'll try to find you something else to wear," I said, then to myself, "I did not think the floor was that dirty."

I found some clothes that an old girlfriend had left. They would be just a little too big for her, but would fit better than mine. I handed the clothes to her.

Not being the least bit modest, she stripped everything off and started putting them on right there. As she was dressing, I turned and went into the kitchen, asking what she wanted for breakfast.

"Breakfast?" she asked.

Here we go again! I thought, shaking my head.

Not bothering to explain, I asked her what she wanted to eat.

"A Glack Fruit," she answered.

"I do not have any Glack Fruit," I said, not even wanting to find out what a Glack Fruit was. "How about an apple?" I got one out of the refrigerator and handed it to her.

"A Glack Fruit!" She grabbed it and starting to munch on it.

As we drove to the auto parts store, I explained what a car was and showed her how it worked. After buying the relay switch, I asked her, "Are you sure this is all that is wrong?"

"I think so. That is what the head engineer said, anyway."

"Do you want to tell me how to get to your ship, or shall I just let you out somewhere and let you walk back?" I wasn't sure whether she wanted me to know where the ship was.

"I will tell you where to go. It is quite far away."

We were about two miles out of town and were driving next to a line of trees when she said suddenly, "Turn here."

As I could not drive through the trees, I parked in a dirt drive, under some trees, that led to a small clearing. "We will have to walk from here," I said.

She led the way. The dense undergrowth and vines clung to us—trying to impede our progress as we walked. After struggling through the undergrowth for about fifteen minutes, we finally came to a small pasture with about twenty head of cattle quietly grazing around—a space ship.

"Oh no! They have returned." She looked at the cattle in alarm. "How are we going to get past them?"

"Easy," I said. "Watch." I took her hand and walked through the herd toward the craft. The cattle walked calmly away from us as we got closer to them.

"How brave you are." She looked at me and smiled.

Well, who was I to argue? I thought, as I shooed the cattle farther away.

As we walked up to the ramp, which had just been lowered, two men came walking down holding palm-sized, silver-colored boxes, with knobs and buttons on them. I presumed these to be weapons.

"I have it, sir," she said excitedly, holding up the relay up to them. She then handed the relay to the older of the two men.

He examined the part and handed it to the other man, whom I presumed was his second-in-command. "Go and have the engineer put this in," he said.

"Are you this Jim Star that I have heard so much about from her?" he asked, staring at me.

"No," I replied. "He is a fictional character I write about."

"What is a . . .*fictional character?*" he asked, staring at me.

Here we go again. I thought. "It means a person or thing that is not real—usually made-up and used as a character in a story or a book.

"What is . . ." he started to ask.

"I'll tell you later." I interrupted.

"Then who are you?" he asked.

"I am the person who made up Jim Star and wrote about him in my books, or Tell Abouts, as you call them," I replied.

"How did you know that this is the part we would need?" he asked, looking at me suspiciously.

"Because I have seen this part before, it is common here on Earth," I answered. I was starting to get tired of the questions.

"I see," he said. "Will you be able to help us?"

"I don't know but I'll try. What would you have me do?" I asked looking at him and then turned to look at Christy, Emulate 3 (the name that I started to think of as hers).

"We are from the planetary system Bright Star, the home of our planet Home Pride," he started explaining. "It is named that because of its appearance—bright and shining. It has two suns that orbit opposite each other, ensuring that we have some light at all times.

"About fifteen Cycles ago, a ship landed on our planet. The beings inside asked for safe asylum. We naturally gave it to them. Little did we know the trouble that this would eventually cause." He motioned for us to ascend the ramp.

I had to interrupt him. I didn't understand what a Cycle was. After some explanation I realized that their Cycle was very similar to our year.

"These beings lived on our planet for about five Cycles when they started demanding that we change our ways. First it was just small things, like observing their holidays and holy days. No one thought anything about it. Then they started forcing their culture on us—like eating or not eating certain things and showing respect a particular way. Then they formed MAMI and made more and more demands from our government.

"It was not long after MAMI was formed that they had taken over control of our government. They started telling us how to dress and even what to wear. Of course, many of us objected. They backed off for a while, but soon started in again.

"Around this time, we noticed that some of us who disagreed with these beings and openly objected started to disappear. They would reappear several Short Cycles later with completely different attitude toward the foreign beings."

Again, I had to interrupt. What the heck was a Short Cycle? I then discovered it was a week.

The captain continued, "We soon got too scared to criticize them and started holding secret meetings in hiding. It did not take long before they discovered and raided these meetings, arresting those they considered troublemakers.

"That is when we realized we were in deep trouble and decided to see if we could find help. We left the opposition movement to continue the fight, and we ended up here. Can you help us? They may have even followed us here," the captain asked me.

The first mate, whom I immediately started to thinking of as Jeff walked in saying, "The relay fits, sir. Now all we have to do is test it." He walked to the controls and looked at the captain for permission.

"Try moving it under . . . those." He pointed to some trees across the clearing.

I followed his gaze. "Under those trees?" I asked.

"Yes," he nodded. "Under those trees. Also activate the Hiding Device. We may have been followed."

We had no sooner gotten under the trees and activated the Hiding Device when a blip appeared on the radar screen.

"It is them." The navigator, whom I had started to think of as Nash, said with concern in his voice, "How did they find us so fast?"

"They haven't yet," I said. "Will the invisibility screen . . . or the Hiding Device . . . work with the ramp down?"

"The what?" The captain looked confused.

"The Hiding Device and the ramp," I replied pointing to the ramp we were standing on.

"Yes, they will work," he answered.

"Lower the ramp," I said. "I have a plan." I turned toward Christy." Not even stopping to think, I asked, "Will you come with me Christy?"

She looked at me strangely. "Who is this Christy?"

"You are," I said looking at her. "Unless you'd rather I call you Emulate 3."

"That is my name, but I like Christy better." She answered as we took off down the ramp. "What is your plan?"

"Well, we will walk through the trees like we had been . . . talking . . . to each other. I'll mess up our clothing or pretend to look for something, and then we'll get in my car and leave."

"Why would we do that?"

"Hopefully they will think we were the blip they saw—if they saw one—and not your ship."

"Sounds like a good plan to me," she said as she smiled.

"Act scared when you see their ship. Here on Earth we do not know they exist," I said quietly, looking up at the horizon.

As we pulled out from under the trees where we had parked, the alien ship flew past us low overhead, then veered off in a different direction.

We pulled out and watched as a pickup pulled alongside of us. "Did you see that?" the driver asked.

"Yes, what was it?" I answered.

"I'm not sure. It looked like a flying spaceship of some sort. I got some pictures though." He waved his camera. "It looked like it was looking for something."

I agreed as he drove away.

"What do we do now?" Christy asked.

"We go back to your ship and make some plans." I said as I reversed the car and parked under some trees. We walked back to the ship to where we "thought" the ship had been—but did not see it. After searching for quite a while, we did find it—by almost tripping on the ramp.

We walked up the ramp into the bay or cargo bay. Captain Savoy was waiting for us.

"That was a fine diversion you thought of. It sure seemed to work."

"Yes, but I am not sure they were completely fooled. You will have to move your ship anyway. The driver of the pickup truck will tell the police what he saw, and they will search this whole area. Christy and I will drive my car back to my house and meet you later."

"Why would Emulate 3 have to go with you?" asked Captain Savoy.

"Now maybe you see why I like Christy better." Christy giggled

"Yes," I said, smiling. I turned to the Captain. "She will have to go with me because the driver saw her and will tell the police. If they stop us we will have to answer a lot of questions. I also want to take my car home so that it does not draw attention parked here. She can contact you later and tell you where to meet us. She does have some type of communication device doesn't she?"

As I descended the ramp, I saw the cattle had started grazing closer to the ship. When we stepped outside of the Hiding Device's range of influence, the cattle all took off the other way. Paying no attention to them, we walked to the car and I opened the door for her.

"Why did you do that? I can open doors by myself." She sounded somewhat abated.

"Because here, opening a car door is the polite thing to do."

I walked to the other side, got in, and started the car. As I drove away I saw a black van on top of a hill a half mile away. Not stopping to see who it might be, I kept driving.

CHAPTER 2

We reached the house without seeing anyone. I pulled the car into the garage and shut the door. I looked out toward the road as the black van drove past.

We entered the house, and I quickly gathered the things we would need. Then we went out the back door, locking the house behind us.

"Where will we go?" Christy was looking around as we entered the woods behind my house.

"I have a cabin up on the mountain a few miles from here. I thought we could go there and you could contact your ship and have them meet us there. I have a few things at the cabin that may help us." I looked over my shoulder at her.

Walking through the flowers that grew between the tree line and my house, I kept glancing over my shoulder to make sure we were not being followed, but also to make sure Christy was keeping up. She seemed to not be used to walking on hard ground. But mostly—I liked watching her walk. The way her body moved while she walked was mesmerizing. Seeing that she was keeping up, I soon suspected she was in better shape than I was. However, she was still having a rough time over the rocky ground, and I started walking slower—but still kept up a good pace.

Before long, I found a fallen log and sat down to rest, telling her it was so I could catch my breath. She looked at me sheepishly, not really believing me, but did not complain as she sank down on the log. As we sat there, catching our breath, I asked her if she had heard from her ship, not stopping to think I would have heard it if she had.

"No." She reached into a pocket of her shorts. The shorts looked like a second skin and did not seem like they could even have a pocket — they were so tight. In fact, they were so tight you could see . . . almost everything. "I should receive a message soon though," she said, looking at her communication device.

As soon as she had said that the unit buzzed. She answered it, smiling as she did.

"Yes sir," she answered.

"Where are you? We have not been able to track you since you left Steve's house," came a gruff reply.

"We are walking through the . . . trees . . . behind Steve's . . . house . . . headed for his . . . cabin . . . up the . . . mountain." She looked to me, as for confirmation that she was right.

"I have them, sir," said Gasser 21, or Nash, the navigator/radio man. "How soon will you be at your . . . cabin?"

Looking at her I said, "About an hour."

She relayed the information to him. When the reply came back about a minute later, it surprised us as the Captain said, "OK. We will meet you there."

That's when I found out that Captain Savoy (the name I gave to the captain) was Commander Aggo 1, the man MAMI was looking for. As I would later find out, he was the leader of the opposition.

"Well, what are you waiting for? We will not get there by just sitting here," Christy said, as she jumped up and started walking. Her breasts bounced as she as she walked. "Let's go. We only have an hour."

We arrived at the cabin in less than fifty minutes. I unlocked the door and we went into the dark, deserted cabin. I found a candle I had left on the table and lit it.

As the candle dimly lit the interior of the cabin, I went to get my kerosene lamp, which I had set on the dresser off to one side of the room. I lit the lamp and set it on the counter next to the stove. Then I went to the closet and got my hunting bow and all the arrows I had, laying them on the table so they were handy if I needed them. Christy and I then sat at the table and waited.

It wasn't long before we heard a strong wind start blowing outside. We hurried to the door, threw it open, and watched as the ship materialized in the clearing.

The ramp came down and the first officer, Jeff, stood at the top yelling for us to hurry. As we ran to the ship, three men came running out of the woods with their short-barreled, large-caliber weapons drawn, yelling for us to stop. When we didn't stop, one of them took a shot at us. It glanced of the ship, just inches from Jeff, who thought quickly and ducked back in the ship—out of sight.

I dropped my packs, notched an arrow in my bow, drew and fired an arrow, hitting the shooter in the shoulder, causing him to miss his shot completely.

The shooter dropped his weapon and clutched his shoulder where the arrow was protruding. He fell to his knees screaming—pleading for the other two to help him. When they turned to look at him, I shot off another arrow, just grazing him.

Grabbing my pack, I sprinted for the ramp, making it just as it started to close. The ship took off so fast we were all knocked to the floor, resulting in a jumbled mess of arms and legs.

I had landed on Christy. Being careful where I placed my hands, I carefully got up. We walked toward the bridge and arrived just as Captain Savoy was orderings to Nash to lose the MAMI ship that had just appeared on the horizon

The captain looked at me. "Do you know of any way to lose them?"

"We could try diving into the ocean. The water." I saw the blank look on his face.

"It is only a few miles away," I said, pointing to the ocean on the horizon. "Will not the Hiding Device hide us?" I asked

"Not now that they have found us," he answered.

"But it will hide us from everyone else, won't it?"

"Yes." He then realized why I had asked. "Turn it on!" he commanded Jeff.

As we cleared the coast I said, "We will have to go several hundred yards out before it is deep enough to hide us."

Once we were far enough out, we started a gentle glide into the ocean. As we struck the water we sent up a wave large enough to almost swamp the trawler that was fishing nearby. Passing under the trawler, we caught its nets and dragged the boat back several hundred yards until the nets broke and it stopped.

The fisherman on that boat must have had one H---- of a story to tell about "the one that got away" when he made it back to port.

As the ship settled to the bottom, we waited for the MAMI ship to stop looking for us. We had to be still since any movement under water would cause a small wake, giving the MAMI an idea where we were.

While we waited, I asked Captain Savoy how big a force they had to fight the MAMI with.

"What do you mean by the word force?" he asked, looking at me somewhat concerned.

"How many men do you have currently to fight the MAMI?"

"That is what I was afraid you meant." The concern did not leave his face. "Well . . . right now we have one thousand twenty-one people . . . with you." He looked at me with a sly grin on his face. "But we can get more hopefully," he said more to himself than to me.

"I hope so," I said under my breath. I hoped he was right.

"There will be a lot of people joining us when we start fighting. I hope it does not come to that though," he said.

"I hope not too. It will take a lot of people." Which turned out to be wrong.

We waited for twelve hours before finally rising to the surface, slowly . . . just breaking the surface so we could use our radar to check for the other ship.

"Where to sir?" Nash asked the captain but looked at me.

"How fast can we get to the far side of the moon?" I asked.

"The moon?" he asked

"The small planet-like object in the sky." I pointed up.

"Two minutes," Nash answered with confidence.

"Then make it so." I looked toward the captain. "When we get there we can look for someplace to hide."

Captain Savoy looked at me then turned to Nash. "Make it so." Glancing at me and grinning. "I like that saying. I think I will start using it," he said.

Two minutes later we were gliding about a hundred feet over the dark and foreboding surface of the dark side of the Earth's moon, trying to spot a depression or cave in which to hide.

"There!" exclaimed Jeff, pointing to a depression in the surface. "Will that work?"

I looked at what appeared to be a large depression, about two thousand feet long and five hundred feet long and about six hundred feet deep.

"Yes," I said. "That should work just fine."

As we descended into the depression, a cave suddenly appeared in the wall, looking almost wide enough for the ship.

"That would be better." I pointed to the cave. "Can you get the ship in there?"

"I can try." Nash steered the craft toward the cave. Then, as an afterthought, looked at the captain, who nodded and said, "Make it so."— a slight smile just starting to show on his lips.

Nash, very carefully, proceeded to guide the ship into the cave, with mere inches to spare on each side.

Settling the ship to the floor of the cave, I said, "I could not have done better myself."

Nash looked at me. "You can pilot this ship?"

I grinned and said, "No . . . that is just a saying that means you did a good job."

He looked at me and grinned, and then went back to doing whatever he had to do to shut the ship down, making it harder to detect.

"Now we wait," the captain said, looking around at everyone.

"How long do you think we will have to wait?" I asked. Just then a small tremor ran through the ship.

"What was that?" I asked, looking around. Dishes and small chairs started to rattle, causing everyone else to look around also.

"Nothing," replied Nash, looking at his instruments. "Just the ship settling"

"I hope you're right," I said, looking around the ship.

A few minutes later, another tremor rippled through the ship. "OK!" I yelled, looking at Nash, who was checking his instruments again.

"If you say so, I still do not believe you though."

At that moment, a young woman, about twenty-one or -two, whom I thought I had glimpsed earlier when Christy had shown me the ship, came walking onto the bridge. "Food's ready," she said.

I just stood staring at her, thinking . . . how much she looked like Christy, but how much better looking she was, standing in just a pair of short shorts. Her short, light brunet hair came to her shoulders. She was petite— about five foot two, yet muscular, with the grace and movements of a deer.

I looked at Christy as she walked off the bridge, glancing over her shoulder at me.

"I will introduce you later when we eat," she said, still smiling.

"Was I that obvious?"

"Yes!" Everyone on the bridge all exclaimed.

"Come on let us eat," Christy said. She took my arm and held it to her chest as we walked to the galley.

Another tremor, slightly stronger than the ones before, shuttered through the ship.

We proceeded into the galley and sat down to a very . . . interesting . . . meal. It looked like nothing I had ever seen. When I tasted it though, I found it tasted extremely good.

As Christy and I were finishing our meal, the Christy look-alike placed two more plates in front of us..

"This is Emulate 2, my sister, my older sister," she said, smiling at Emulate 2.

"I am not that much older," she said, suddenly going quiet and playfully slapping at her sister.

"This is Steve Stevenson," Christy said to her sister. "He . . . wrote . . . the Jim Star novels.

"What is a novel?" she asked, smiling at me.

"It is a Tell About that I wrote about a fictional character." I stared at her large blue eyes.

"What is a . . . ?"

"A person who is not real, but made up, to be portrayed in a Tell About . . . book . . . to give the reader someone to relate to." Christy said, trying to sound as if she knew what she was talking about.

"I still do not understand," Emulate 2 said to her sister. "Oh! I was going to ask what a . . . *book* . . . was."

"I said it was it was a Tell About," Christy said.

"Would you tell me what a . . . *fictional character* . . . is?" She asked me.

"Yes," I said. "Later."

"What is later?"

"A time in the future when we have more time to talk," I answered.

"Maybe we should show him what is met by *talking*." Said Christy looking slyly at me and then at her sister.

"Hmm . . . maybe we should." She looked at Christy and then back at me with a gleam in her eye.

As Emulate 2 turned to leave, another larger tremor shook the ship, knocking her into my lap. I placed my arms around her waist, under her breasts, to keep her from falling to the floor.

"Are you all right?" I asked.

"Yes." She tried to twist around but ended up even closer to me. She looked back over her shoulder.

She stared at me for a few seconds. "You can let go now."

"What if I don't want to?" I gazed into her deep blue eyes

"Well I think you had better before I get in trouble for not doing my job," she said shyly.

"OK, Abbrelle."

"Who is this Abbrelle?" she asked hotly. "Is she your girlfriend?"

"I hope she will be," I said, still gazing at her. "But for now she is just you."

Christy was grinning. "He does not like our names, Sis. He thinks his names are better."

"What is wrong with our names?" she said coolly this time.

"Nothing," I said. "It's just that my names are easier for me to remember. And I can keep you all straight easier. Besides, your names sound strange to me."

"Well yours sounds strange to me to," said Abbrelle. "And this is something you will explain later to me?"

"Yes," I said, reluctantly letting her go.

"Seems like you two are going to have a lot to 'talk' about, later." Nash said, standing behind us.

As she stood up another tremor shook the ship, causing her to fall into my lap again. This time I put my arms around her . . . pulling her close.

"I am sorry," she said with a big smile on her lips.

"I'm not." I held her tighter.

Just then Jeff came into the room. "You are wanted on the bridge, Mr. Steve."

"Sorry I have to go," I said, slowly releasing my hold on her.

"I like the name Abbrelle," she said.

As I was stepping onto the bridge, another shock wave shook the ship causing everyone to grab hold of something or someone to maintain their balance. The tremors were stronger now. We could hear rocks falling on the hull of the ship.

"That was close," Jeff said looking around the bridge for damage.

"Do you have any idea what is going on?" asked Captain Savoy, looking at me.

Even though I had no idea, I took a guess and said, "They are probably just shooting into any possible hiding place, trying to hit us with a lucky shot.

He nodded his head as if in agreement as the shock waves let up.

We waited five minute, listening.

"Do you always keep it this warm in here?" I started to undo some of the buttons of my shirt.

"Yes. This is the average temperature of our planet. One hundred five of your degrees, with seventy per cent humidity."

"No wonder you dress like you do."

"Would you like something to drink?" he asked.

"Yes, please." I undid the rest of the buttons on my shirt and removed it.

Nash, pressing a button on his console said, "Emulate 2, would you please bring some refreshments to the bridge."

When she walked in a minute later, now topless and smiling at me, she said to all on the bridge, "Would you please call me Abbrelle?"

Passing the refreshments around, she looked at me and said with a gleam in her eyes, "Will there be anything else," she turned toward the captain, "Sir?"

"No that will be all for now . . . um . . . Abbrelle," he replied with a knowing smile as he watched her watching me.

She turned and left the bridge with a slight wiggle of her hips and a smile on her lips—a smile that had not been there before.

"I think our . . . little Abbrelle finds someone . . . interesting. I guess that ends the 'talking' with her," Jeff said looking at me.

"What is this 'talking' you keep talking about?" I asked.

"You will find out in due time. I think very soon." He grinned at me.

"We have to figure out a way to get the MAMI to quit shooting and stop looking for us." I said as another tremor shook the ship, causing more rocks fall on the ship. "Before they hit us! They must have a good idea where we are," I said as the MAMI continued firing in our ship's vicinity.

Suddenly it became dead–quiet. The firing had stopped. However, the vibration that we felt of our ship told us the enemy ship was landing close by.

Does this ship have any armament?" I asked.

"What do you mean by armament?" the captain asked.

"A weapon to shoot at them with," I said.

"No," he replied. "All we can do is throw rocks or use the Sleep Ray Device on them. But you have to be close to use the device.

"How close?"

"About twenty five meters or less."

"Is the device portable?" I asked.

"Somewhat," the captain said.

"Do you have any space suits?" I asked.

"Space suits?"

"Yes, a suit I can use to go out in a vacuum in."

"Oh, yes . . . here." He handed me a belt. "This will last for five minutes. If you need more time you can carry a canister with you."

Thinking I would need at least that much time, I asked for the two-hour canister.

Jeff walked to the locker and pulled out a half-gallon size canister and handed it to me. He then showed me how to use it.

"What are you are going to do?" asked Christy as she walked onto the bridge.

"I am going to capture that ship," I said looking at her.

"Not without me you're not!" she exclaimed, both hands on her hips.

"Or me!" exclaimed Abbrelle too. "You're not getting yourself killed trying to act brave before we have had a chance to be 'talking' with you," she said defiantly. She stood looking at me with her closed fists on her hips.

Christy nodded her head in agreement. "Besides we can help."

I looked at them and said, "No, you cannot. I can handle this by myself." I tried to sound strong and macho.

"Yes, we can!" they said in unison—their hands still on their hips and defiance still on their faces.

"There is no arguing with a woman, let alone two. Besides they are both fully qualified for this type of work," said Captain Savoy, stopping any further argument on my part.

"I guess not," I said, looking at them both standing with very determined and defiant looks on their pretty faces. Looking at Jeff I said, "I guess we will need two more canisters—and belts. By the way how do you work these?"

As he was getting the necessary equipment from the locker, Abbrelle said, "See, you do need me . . . if only to explain how things work." She sounded excited.

They proceeded to show me how the canisters attached to the belts—belts which turned out to be standard-issue to all crew members. The belts had force fields that acted as space suits and also provided protection against light weapons. All you had to do was carry extra air if you were going to use the suits for more than five minutes.

"What is the plan?" Abbrelle asked, as we started for the ramp.

"Well first of all, would you both please put shirts on? You are distracting me." They both stood there without anything on above the waist.

"What does he mean by putting shirts on?" asked Abbrelle.

"He means the type of covering I was wearing when I came back to the ship."

"We do not have anything like that to put on!" exclaimed Abbrelle. "We will just have to go like this," she said, smiling at me as she shook her chest. "Besides we fight better like this."

"OK." I tried not to look at their bare chests.

Jeff dragged the Sleep Ray Device onto the ramp.

"You do know how to use it don't you?" I asked Abbrelle.

"Yes, I have used it before and I'll be careful. I thought you said you could handle this by yourself?" She gave me a smug look.

"Have you come up with a plan yet?" Christy asked.

"Of course he has." Abbrelle gave Christy a cool look, and then turned toward me. "You have, have you not?"

"I think so," I said. "We'll just go and take the ship away from them."

I quickly explained how I would just walk up to the ship and use the Sleep Ray to overtake the MAMI. As we preparing the Sleep Ray for transport, I was thinking that, truth be told, I really had no plan, yet.

When we got the Sleep Ray ready, we descended the ramp. Abbrelle and I carried it between us using straps that were around our shoulders.

Once we had cleared the ramp and were in the cave, we were hit with another small aftershock caused by MAMI's random firing. A few small rocks and some dust fell on us in the light gravity.

I was pleasantly surprised at how well the force field worked as a space suit.

CHAPTER 3

We were looking at amount of stone and debris that had been knocked down around the ship. This would eventually have to be cleared away before the ship could leave again, a job of many hours.

As Christy walked down the ramp she looked around at the rubble. "It looks like we will be here for a while."

"Come on," I said "Let us get this to the surface."

The Sleep Ray was portable, but barely. It took all three of us to get it to the cave entrance. The ground leading out of the cave was treacherous; we had to walk over, around, and in some cases through piles of rocks.

Outside the entrance of the cave, I noticed a fairly good trail leading up in a roundabout way to the top. The trail was along a sheer wall. The wall was pretty level except for one spot where it rose about four feet in.

I turned to Christy." Do you have some rope in the ship?"

"Rope? What is that?" she asked.

"A length of many cords twisted together so it is strong. Something we can use to pull the Sleep Ray up that wall."

She looked at the wall for a few seconds, then said, "Yes, I will be right back." She returned with a short length of what looked like light rope.

"Will this work?" she asked, handing me a length of the rope.

"Yes, what do you call this? On Earth we call it rope. I hope it will be strong enough."

"Here we call it tie down." Christy answered. She smiled, looking pleased with herself.

I tied the rope to the Sleep Ray and we started to drag it up the so-called trail. When we reached the stone wall we had to struggle harder to get it up. The rest of the walk to the top was fairly easy. Once at the top, we stopped just short of the crest.

We looked around very carefully; we knew the MAMI ship knew we were close. Our cautiousness paid off because the enemy ship had sat down just fifty meters away.

"Are we close enough?" asked Christy.

"No, we need to get closer," Abbrelle answered.

"Maybe we could get over to that pile of rocks," I said, pointing to the rocks about fifteen or twenty meters from the ship.

As we moved very carefully toward our destination rocks, we kept a close watch on the ship for any signs of movement.

Once we reached the rocks undetected, Abbrelle tapped me on the shoulder and shrugged hers, giving me that look that says, *What now?*

I held up my hand; now we wait. After about fifteen minutes, the ramp of the ship lowered and five men came out, looking all around. Satisfied, they turned toward our direction.

I fired the Sleep Ray. The men all fell just as they stepped off the bottom of the ramp.

"Do you think we got them all?" asked Abbrelle.

"I hope so, but I doubt it." I answered. Just then ten more men ran down the ramp to see what had happened to their companions.

"What do we do know?" asked Christy.

"We punt," I said.

The women both crouched there in their tight, short shorts— shorts that were now so tight you could make out . . . everything, as they crouched with their legs partly open. "Later," I said looking at Abbrelle . . . as she crouched their staring at me.

"What would they do if you stepped out with this in your hand?" I held up a square shaped rock that looked like it could be a weapon.

"I do not know," Abbrelle said, looking at the rock. I held it out to her.

"Abbrelle . . . go over there—quietly." I pointed to the right side of a rock pile. Handing Christy a similar rock as Abbrelle's, I said, "And you go to the other side of the pile. Both of you stand up when I tell you to."

Once they made their way to their assigned spots, they stopped and turned, watching me. I turned the Sleep Ray up to the maximum power setting. When I looked toward the MAMI ship, I saw that fifteen more men descending down the ramp to check on the fallen men. Several had their weapons out, keeping watch.

After checking the settings and aim of the Sleep Ray, I fired. The result was instantaneous. All twenty-five men dropped to the ground, lying there with the other five.

We waited a few minutes and then I motioned for Abbrelle to stand up and show herself. She stood up and held out the weapon that really just a rock, acting like she had shot the men who were lying on the ground. Shortly, with weapons out and ready, ten more men ran down the ramp, some of them tripping over the fallen men, all yelling and raising their weapons—ready to fire at Abbrelle. Right then Christy stood up and acted like she was ready to start firing at them. That was my cue to fire the Sleep Ray. The men all fell, making it look as if Christy had shot them with a wide dispersing ray.

When no one else had come out of the ship after ten more minutes, I carefully walked up to the nearest unconscious man and picked up his weapon. I motioned for Abbrelle and Christy to collect all of the other weapons and place them well out of the men's reach, should they regain consciousness before we could figure out what to do with them.

After each of us had selected a weapon for ourselves, as the captain and first mate were the only ones with weapons on our ship, I had the women follow me up the ramp.

Reaching the top of the ramp, the man I had hit in the shoulder with my arrow at the cabin opened the hatch leading into the ship. His arm was in a sling. "You may as well come up," he said, "I cannot stop you." He stepped back and allowed us entry to the ship.

"How long is their oxygen supply?" I asked, pointing to the men lying unconscious on the ground.

"About two hours," he replied looking at me surly.

"Reaol 10, it is nice to see you. I thought they had put you in a rehabilitation camp after they captured you," said Abbrelle, smiling and staring at him intensely.

"Emulate 2! Emulate 3!" He exclaimed, running to them and giving each a big hug. "It is good to see you. I was afraid I would not see you again. Then I finally convinced them I had accepted their ways, and they sent me on this mission as a test. Are you taking over this ship? It is better equipped to fight them. I can join you now. I have been trying to think of a way I could. I have been trying to stop them."

"Slow down!" I said. "How do we know you are telling the truth and are not just trying to stop us? You could always turn on us later."

"I guess you do not know," he said, looking pleadingly at both girls. "We had better get them in here and tied up before they wake."

I looked at Christy and said, "I have a better idea. Go back to our ship and bring some personnel back with you. Bring Captain Savoy too." She left to return to our ship as Reaol 10 and I had started tying the unconscious men up.

Abbrelle had not said a word since she first spoke with Reaol 10 but had kept a close eye on him the whole time.

Captain Savoy arrived with Jeff and ten others; they looked at the men we had tied up. He stopped and looked strangely at Reaol 10.

"It does not look like you need our help. So why did you ask us to come over?" Glancing around then looking back at Reaol 10—"Do we need to do something with him?" he asked.

"Not yet. He says he wants to join us," I replied. "Do you think we can trust him?"

"YES!" exclaimed both Abbrelle and Christy.

"He was a good man before the sent him to rehabilitation," he said, looking intently at Reaol 10.

"They tried to rehabilitate me but it did not work, sir," Reaol 10 said, looking at the captain. "I fooled them into thinking it had."

"Ok." The captain looked over at Abbrelle and Christy with a questioning look. "If they speak for you, I will trust you."

"Yes sir, we will take responsibility for him." Abbrelle said with no hesitation.

Looking at Abbrelle with a curious look, Christy said to her, "We will talk about it later."

I then told the captain of my plan to change ships with the prisoners.

"Yes," he said. "That might just work." He rubbed his chin thoughtfully.

As we were talking, one of the men that had first come down the ramp opened his eyes and looked around. He saw his comrades lying on the ground tied up, some starting to awaken—the man next to him acting as if he was about to moan in pain. The conscious man quickly nudged the other to silence him, causing him to lie still.

The man, still in pain, looked at his companion with an unasked question dying on his lip. It did not take but a second for him to realize what was going on. His comrade motioned for him to be quiet.

The man who had first awakened looked at Commander Aggo 1 who was watching the rest of the tied up men. His opportunity came a minute later when the commander turned to look at one of his men. He quickly sat up, drew a knife, and threw it at the commander.

Just as he threw it, Christy saw the movement and yelled, "Look Out!"

At her shout the commander dropped to the deck, the knife flying just barely over his shoulder as he did. The rest of us, except for Christy, Abbrelle, and Reaol 10, did the same. Christy immediately sprang into action by jumping over prone bodies and striking a blow to the knife-thrower's body, knocking him back, then slamming a well-placed strike to the man's throat with her hand, causing him to gasp for air through his crushed larynx.

Abbrelle, straddling one man, hit another, causing him to fall back and drop his knife that he was about to throw at Christy. Abbrelle grabbed his arm and rolled him over, pulling up on his arm back so hard that she dislocated his shoulder, causing him to scream in pain and curl up in to a ball.

Christy and Abbrelle both instantly drew their weapons and aimed toward the rest of the MAMI group . . . some of whom were starting to show signs of movement.

Reaol 10 ran to Christy, his hand out. She handed her weapon to him after pausing for a second, then nodded her head at him.

"I see you have not lost your edge," Reaol said. "You both are still as good as you ever were. We still can make a good team when I get better, Sister."

The man Christy had struck lay on the deck, coughing and gagging, fighting for breath through his damaged larynx.

Both Christy and Abbrelle turned to me as I said, "I guess you two are not just the two helpless little girls I thought you to be."

"No!" exclaimed Captain Savoy, smiling at me. "They are not just two helpless little girls. They are my personal bodyguards. They have been training their whole lives for this," he said, looking at them with pride.

"Your personal bodyguards?" I was stunned.

"Yes. I am Commander Aggo 1, leader of the opposition against the MAMI," he said, looking at me. "I have trained them for this their whole lives."

"No, we are not helpless. We, with our brother here," she said, pointing to Reaol 10, "were the commander's personal guards until Reaol 10 was captured."

"And here I have been trying to protect you. Silly me!" I said sheepishly.

"We really do appreciate the effort," said Abbrelle, looking at me with the same doe-like eyes her sister had used when we first met.

"Ohhh! Is that the way it is?" said her brother, smiling at her. "Is that why you like it when you are called Abbrelle? I suppose you will stop 'talking' to me and other men now?"

"Yes! That is why she likes being called Abbrelle, and I like being called Christy. I may stop 'talking' to you to," Christy exclaimed hotly.

"You may as well get use to it. He calls me Captain Savoy," the commander said with a grin.

"And me, Jeff," the first officer spoke up.

"And me, Nash," added the navigator, all looking at Reaol 10 with a smile on their lips.

CHAPTER 4

"What are you going to call me?" asked Reaol 10.

"I do not know you yet. But it will come to me," I said to him as I turned looking at the prisoners.

"Do not worry. He will think of something," Christy said, grinning at him.

"I am sorry, but this wound has really slowed me down," he said to the commander, looking at me with disdain.

"You were shooting at Jeff," I said, looking at him the same way.

"No I was not, I missed, did I not? If you had not shot me, I would have missed by just enough so that no questions would have been asked." He glared at me. "I had to make it look good. I had gone through retraining, remember!"

"How was I to know?" I said. "It looked to me like you were trying to shoot him. Besides, you missed and no questions were asked, were they?"

"No, but now I have this wounded arm. . . ."

"It looked to me like you were shooting at Jeff too," Christy said, glaring at him.

Reaol 10 just looked at both of us, then turned to the commander saying, "I would have missed."

"Forget it for now," said the commander. "What are we going to do with these prisoners?" The prisoners were all sitting on the deck.

"Well . . . " I started to say when Nash interrupted: "If it was up to me, I would put them out on the surface with little air."

"Have them take a long walk on a short plank," I said looking at him.

"What?" he asked.

"Just an old Earth saying—means the same thing. I think we should place them on our ship and take theirs. Who knows how long it will take them to get our ship out of there with all the rocks that fell around it. We could use their ship to return to your planet, using Reaol 10 here to get us through the enemy. We can work on the finer points of the plan en route."

"Sounds good to me," the commander said. "Make it so."

Turning to Jeff he said, "Go and tell the rest of the crew of the plan. Gather all of our belongings and get the ship ready for its new crew.

With that he left, taking some of the personnel that had come over with him.

I looked at the prisoners as they sat and said to them, "We are going to take you to the other ship and . . . Aw hell, you heard. Get up and let's go. Remember, if you try to run, we will not come after you. What you are carrying is all the air you have."

"You will die before any help could possible reach you," Reaol 10 said, looking at the prisoners.

They all got up slowly and with the commander taking the lead started walking down the trail Jeff had just used to get back to our ship.

At the drop-off, the commander stopped and said, "How will we fly that ship? None of us know how. It's the newest model."

"But I do," said Reaol 10. "I know how to fly this ship and so do my sisters. I have been watching your pilot, noting all the things he has done, so get going. Um, where to?" he asked looking at the drop.

"Abbrelle, will you show him the way?" I asked, looking at her.

"Be happy to," she said as she walked in front of him and stepped off the drop, landing softly, and started toward the cave.

Reaching the ship, we met Jeff at the bottom of the ramp, having just placed some of the crew's belongings there. "Wait a minute," he said, holding up a hand. "The crew is just finishing moving all of our things." Just as he finished talking the last of the crew exited the ship with more belongings.

"Will food and air be a problem for them?" I asked, having just thought of it.

"That will not be a problem," answered Jeff, matter-of-factly.

We were watching the prisoners finish boarding our old ship when the commander shouted, "Come on, grab your things and let us leave them to their fate." Then he closed the ramp.

"Will they be able to call for help?" I asked the commander as we walked back.

"Yes, after they fix the radio perhaps," he said, holding up a frequency chip and some other electronics from the radio.

"Are there other chips on board?" I asked.

"Somewhere, maybe," was the answer I got from him—with a smile.

When we arrived at our new ship, the crewmen we had left on board were just finishing removing the old crew's personal belongings.

"Is there anything we may need to aid us in our deception when we land?" I looked at the pile of . . . things . . . that were being unloaded.

"No," said both Nash and Reaol 10, who had been helping to move the items out.

"There will be something we need. There always is," I said.

As we boarding the ship and began putting things away, we found we had more room on this ship and would not have to sleep two to a sleep pad.

As we prepared to lift off, we felt the ship shudder and saw some dirt drift from the cave where our old ship was.

"Well, it looks like they tried to move the ship," Nash said to the commander. "It does not look like that went to well. It had a thin hull, you know."

The commander watched the dust still drifting up from the cave and said, "Let's go."

"They made their bed. Now they can lie in it," I said.

"What?" the commander asked, turning to me.

"Just an old Earth saying, meaning they made their mess, now they have to live with it."

Having left the moon three weeks ago and not knowing the speed of the ship, I went to the commander and asked how much longer it would take to reach his planet.

"We will be there in about another day," he said, looking at me a little concerned, "if everything goes well. Why? Is the enclosed space getting to you?"

"A little," I said back to him—a little more sternly than I had intended.

"You are starting to suffer from what we call Space Sickness." He was looking at me more intently.

"Hmm, claustrophobia." I wanted to change the subject. "How long did it take to find my planet?"

"We had been traveling in this general direction for about a half Cycle. We were checking for possible planets when we heard your radio signals. We decided to investigate, hoping we could find help. Your planet was the first with life that we had found." He continued to look at me. "Why do you not go and work out in the ramp bay. That is the largest free area on the ship. It will help you."

As I turned and stepped from the bridge, I almost ran into both Abbrelle and Christy.

"Where are you going?" Abbrelle asked.

"The commander suggested I go to the ramp bay and work out."

"Oooh," said Christy, recognition dawning of her face. "Space Sickness!" She turned to Abbrelle. "I think we should go and help him work out. Do you not agree, Sister?"

"Yes, I think you may be right. If nothing else, we will get to. . . " Abbrelle said, smiling back at her.

I looked at the two of them standing there grinning wickedly at me, wondering what I had I gotten myself into.

As we headed for the ramp bay, we ran into their brother, Reaol 10.

Noticing that both girls were grinning broadly, he asked where we were headed.

"We are going to the ramp bay to . . . work out . . . with Steve," Christy said, smiling at him.

He gave them a sideways look, smirking a little. "Can I come with you?"

"Well, I suppose if you have to." Abbrelle gave him a dirty look, trying to figure a way to tell him no.

Christy and Abbrelle both walked into the ramp bay ahead of me and stepped quickly to the sides of the hatchway.

When I stepped through, they both tackled me, one from each side, taking me to the floor.

As I lay there with both of them on top of me laughing, Reaol 10 stepped through the hatchway. "What do you think you are doing?"

"What does it look like? We were just showing Steve why he should always look before going through a hatchway." Christy said, smiling as she ran her fingers over my chest.

"Yes," said Abbrelle, rolling off my chest but leaving her hand— lower on my body.

Looking at the women he said, "That is not what it looks like to me." He started to take his shorts off.

Christy stood up and started taking her tight short shorts off too.

I looked at Abbrelle. She was doing the same, sliding her shorts from her feet. "Well, get those clothes off, Steve. Or we will be forced to show you why you should not wear them when you . . . work out." She grabbed me by the waistband of my pants and pulled me close against her. "See now, get them off." Her hands were on her hips, legs spread slightly, as she was looking at me.

"You mean we are going to work out in the NUDE?"

"What is nude?" asked Reaol 10.

"If this is what you call nude, then yes," said Christy. "This is the normal way to work out. We do it like this all the time. It gives your opponent less to hold on to when trying to take you down. It also is easier to move."

"Nude is when you have no clothes on, like now," I said as I dropped the last of my clothing to the floor. "You say you work out like this every day." I turned to Reaol 10. "Reaol, you know I am going to have to find a name for you?"

"My name is Reaol 10, not just Reaol," he said coldly. "Yes. I'm sure you'll find me a name. Now get ready to defend yourself," he said as he stepped back.

"OK. Where do we start?" I asked feeling odd.

"First, we start with warm-up exercises," Abbrelle said, taking charge. She obviously had done this before. Spreading her legs wide, she started doing toe touches. After warming up for about a half hour, she said, "Now we start by finding out what you know. Stand there and I will attack you."

"OK, but I have to warn you . . . I know some judo." I got into a defensive stance.

Abbrelle just looked at me and shook her head. Before I even saw her start to move, she grabbed me by the arm and threw me over her shoulder. I hit the floor hard. Groaning, I looked up at her, bent over me, her breasts in my face as she checked to see if I was all right. She sank down to her knees, over my . . . stomach, still bent over. "Did I hurt you?" she asked, running her hands over my body . . . checking.

"No . . . I guess I don't know as much as I thought I did," I said, groaning as I started to rise. "Shall we continue?"

When I was getting to my feet, she grabbed me and threw me over her shoulder. As she threw me down she turned me over and put her knee in my lower back, grabbed my head, pulled it back, and exposed my throat. She gently jabbed her thumb against it, showing me how easy it would have been for her to kill me.

We continued the workout for at least another hour. The women put me in all kinds of headlocks, leg locks, body holds, and moves that I never knew even existed. They wrapped their legs around me in ways that were quite sexual and for the most part, very painful. They taught me how to do the different holds. I then I would try the holds that I just learned on one of them. Reaol10 also put holds on me, and the women would instruct me how to get out of them.

We continued until I was so tired I had to call it quits. I fell to the floor and rubbed my sore and bruised body.

As we sat Reaol 10 would continue to sneak up and put me into a variety of holds. I could never hear him coming and neither of the girls would help me. They always seemed to be looking the other way when he attacked me. I soon learned to expect an attack whenever they looked the other way, which was most of the time. He continued this until I finally got up to defend myself, which I did with very little success.

"You know," I said once as he came up behind me. "They should have named you Hunter since you move so quietly and quickly. You move like a cat—fast and quiet. You are a natural Hunter.

He looked at me and said, "I like that name. I think I will use it from now on. Thank you."

After we had been working out for about two hours, Captain Savoy came through the hatch and while undressing asked if he could join us. Agreeing, I had to go through all the moves again, with him laughing at me and putting me in a very great many different holds and throws. As he became aware as to how little I knew, he began laughing so hard it brought tears to his eyes.

"I thought from the way you moved and acted you knew a lot more about self-defense," he said, laughing while he wiped the tears from his eyes.

"As you can see, I know just enough to get myself into trouble." I grinned at him.

CHAPTER 5

After we had gone through my humiliating display of self–defense, the commander said to us, "Get dressed. You can carry on with this workout later. We are coming to a Defense Station in about one hour. Reaol 10, you will have to make the contact since I'm not familiar with these new procedures yet.

"My new name is Hunter, sir," he said, glancing at me.

"Fine, I will call you by that name in private, but for now I think we should still use Reaol 10," the captain said, giving him a stern look.

"But I was just an aide on the ship," he said. "I had very little to do with the bridge."

"Be that as it may, I still think you should be the one to contact the MAMI. You know more of their procedures and protocols than I do. I doubt they will recognize me, or any of us for that matter, since this is a completely different Defense Station from the one you were on."

In the time remaining we came up with a fairly plausible reason to give the Defense Station why the captain and most of the crew were missing. When the time came that we would answer their hail, we were confident that our story would hold up and allow us passage to Starbase Outreach. We wanted to eventually contact some other members of the opposition. There were at least two of whom Commander Aggo 1 knew personally, one being a the commander of the base.

As the captain and Hunter waited for the Defense Station to contact us, both were inspecting their uniforms, making sure they accurately depicted the enemy. The hail came through right when it was anticipated, but still took everyone by surprise.

When we answered the hail, we were surprised to hear they were aware of the previous crew's mission. They questioned us and inquired as to the reason that we were returning from the other side of the galaxy so soon. It took about two hours to answer all of their questions. We had to answer many questions with the statement that the information was classified—since we did not know the answers.

CHAPTER 6

"Commander, we have a request that just came in from Surveillance Defense Station Nine asking for permission for the *SS 927-C* to land here," said the young lieutenant standing at attention in her uniform —a uniform that consisted of a top that covered to just above her breasts and a short miniskirt. She saluted the commander as she handed him the communication.

The commander of Starbase Outreach returned her salute and reached for the message with the other hand. "Thank you Lieutenant. Please inform the Defense Station that the message is received and understood. Dismissed."

Opening the communication, he read it. He read it again. After reading it for the third time, he laid it down, looked at it, then picked it up and read it again:

Commander, we have a request from Lieutenant Reaol 10 aboard the SS 927-C to land at your base. He says he has an important message he can only deliver to you personally. He can be contacted on channel 99.3 of your secure S.C. transmitter. We will continue holding the SS 927-C in orbit until further orders from you.

It was signed, Crop 5 Captain, Surveillance Defense Station Nine.

The commander looked at the message again and thought *I know a Reaol 10, but he was sent to reeducation nine months ago for receiving and acting on information from the supposed dissident, Commander Aggo 1. He was his bodyguard and would have known he was being watched.*

The last the commander had heard, Reaol 10 had been sent capture Commander Aggo 1 and return him. Was it not on the 927-C he had left on? The commander thought hard as he looked at the communication in his hand.

If this was a trick, how would they have known about the secure S.C. transmitter and channel 99.3?—a designation that was only known to a few, although Commander Aggo 1 was one of the few who did know. Glancing at the message again, he wondered if it was possible that Reaol 10 had somehow overcome the reeducation and found the commander? No, he did not think that was possible. But still stranger things had happened.

He sat at his desk, thinking. *Well if we are going to beat the MAMI, someone has to take the chance of being wrong.* He knew he would have to wait until he was at home before he could reach the transmitter. He spent the rest of the Wake Period wondering what he was getting himself into.

Gathering his things to leave, Lieutenant Distain 8 knocked on the door, came in, and closed it softly behind her, looking first to make sure no one was there. Turning to the commander, said in hushed tones, "Sir, may I speak, off the record?"

"Yes, one moment." He reached under his desk and threw a hidden switch that activated a White Noise Device hidden there.

"Sir, did that message have anything to do concerning your friend Commander Aggo?" she asked sounding quite concerned. "There are officers here that would like to get evidence that you are helping the dissidents. I know I am talking a chance talking to you about this. But I disagree with the MAMI and I want to help. I hope I have read you right."

The commander, sitting back down at his desk and looking at the young lieutenant in her uniform thoughtfully said, "What makes you think I have or would ever help the dissidents, Lieutenant?"

"Well, I know of your relationship to the commander, and I was hoping that I had not misinterpreted the impression I got. Is there anything I can do to help?" The commander simply stared at her, not saying a word. "I know you may think I am trying to trap you into saying or doing something that will incriminate you, but I assure you that I am not," she said, looking deeply concerned.

Finally, the commander said, "I know your father and I trust him. Let me call and see if he is still in his office and is free to come over. Just remember that if I am wrong about this you will not only take me down but you will also take your father down too." He looked at her intently.

"Yes sir," the young lieutenant said, looking at him very seriously.

" Go back to your desk and keep busy for about a half hour? I will buzz you when he arrives."

"Yes sir," she said. She turned and left the room.

"I hope I did not make a mistake," he said to himself as he picked up the phone to call Major Calm 27, turning off the White Noise Device after he had completed the call.

About a half hour later, there was a knock on his door.

"Yes," answered the commander.

"It's me. Major Calm 27."

"Come in." The commander put down the papers he was working on.

The major walked in, followed closely by his daughter, Lieutenant Distain 8.

"Please sit down." The commander looked at them both with a thoughtful expression on his face as he turned the White Noise Device back on.

"Your daughter has expressed a desire to help against MAMI," he said looking directly at the major. "Can we trust her?"

The major looked at his daughter sitting next to him in her uniform. He then turned back to the commander. "I would trust her with my life."

"That is what we both will be doing," he said back to the major. "OK, I will trust her with my life too. This is what I want you to do." He looked to the lieutenant.

"I want you to get some safe, let me stress the word *safe* quarters for about twenty or twenty-five people. They must not be seen nor is anyone to know where they are once they land.

"How long will you need these quarters for and how soon do you need them, sir?" she asked.

"I am not sure. Let us say two Short Cycles, and I will need them as soon as you can get them, by tomorrow at the latest."

"I will get right on it." She stood and left the room.

"What do you think? Can we trust her?" the commander asked, looking at Distain 8's father.

"Yes sir. I have complete confidence in her," he answered.

"I hope we can. We just put our lives in her hands." With that, he said, "Let us retire to my quarters. I have someone I need to talk to." He shut off the White Noise Device and headed for the door.

When they reached his quarters the commander dismissed his staff for the evening and said to the Major, "Come with me." He led him into a small room off his living quarters through a secret door. The room had a transmitter in it.

After setting the transmitter to the proper channel and allowing it to warm up, he made his call.

CHAPTER 7

"This is Victor calling Rescue—over." He keyed the microphone, knowing that everything he was about to say would be scrambled as it was transmitted.

After a slight pause, the response came.

"This is Rescue—over."

"How can I help you old friend?—over."

"You can buy me a Slovic—over."

"What is a Slovic?" asked the major.

"Just part of the recognition code," the commander said. "It changes with each use. The second letter becomes the first letter for the next word." He turned his head looking at the major intensely. "Now that you know our code names and some the formatting of our code, Major, I trust that you will keep it secret."

"Of course," the major said.

Turning back to the transmitter and keying the microphone, he said, "I have several here. How can I help you, Rescue—over.

The reply came instantly. "We need landing instructions and accommodations for twenty-one personnel—over," said the disembodied voice from the speaker.

"It is being arranged as we speak—over."

"Please give landing instructions to Mr. Nash. Over and out."

"Mr. Nash?" queried Major Calm 27, looking at the commander.

"I presume that is the navigator," was the only answer he received.

Looking at the major, the commander asked, "Will you call the control tower and tell them to land the *SS 927-C* please."

"Immediately," the commander replied.

After the arrangements had been made, there was nothing more for them to do. Sitting back in their chairs, the commander started telling the major who Rescue was and what its arrival would mean.

The next morning, Lieutenant Distain 8 was waiting for the commandeer in his office with a handful of papers, most looked important.

"Come with me," he said passing her. He walked through the door and set his things on the desk. The lieutenant quickly handed him the papers, then closed the door.

"Sir," she started to say, but stopped as he held up his hand.

He went around the desk and reached under it, turning on the White Noise Device. Then he turned to her and asked, "What do you have to report?"

Nodding her head in understanding, she said, "Sir, I have made all of the necessary arrangements and the . . . guests . . . will be comfortable with the accommodations I have made for them."

"Very well Lieutenant. You will meet our guests at the landing zone at twenty hundred hours and escort them to their accommodations. Will that fit into your plans?" he asked as he sat down.

"Yes sir, I will make it work in to them," she replied.

Reaching under the desk, he flipped the White Noise Device off. "Now," he said, laying the papers on his desk and picking up a pen and some paper. Looking at the papers and shuffling them loudly, he started to write a note for the young lieutenant. He handed her the finished note, still moving he papers as if he was reading them and making notes. "You will take care of this immediately," he said as she read the note. She nodded her head in understanding. He continued to read through the papers on his desk.

After some time, he reached under the desk and flipped on the White Noise Device again, saying, "We are bugged."

"Yes sir, I figured as much."

CHAPTER 8

After receiving the landing instructions from the Defense Station for the landing, Captain Savoy/Commander Aggo 1, said to all who were standing on the bridge, "Prepare to be boarded for inspection. Hopefully, then we will be able to land. You all need to replace your uniforms with MAMI uniforms before we are boarded." He looked at the crew standing in their short shorts. He sat down in the command chair with a heavy sigh. "I hope this works.'

As we waited for them to board, we watched a small craft move slowly toward us. Clearly in no hurry, sliding up to our boarding hatch, the two vessels slowly coupled and the hatchways were opened. We were boarded. They all held their weapons at the ready.

The captain of the MAMI ship strolled slowly over to Commander Aggo 1. He looking at him and then at Reaol 10, who was standing next to him. "What happened to Captain Hergo 10? I thought he was the captain of this ship?"

Commander Aggo 1 looked at him and said, "We ran into trouble. He was killed trying to capture the instigators along with several members of the crew."

The captain turned to Reaol 10, having recognized him as having gone through reeducation. "You went through reeducation, is that correct?"

"Yes sir," he replied looking at him with a straight face.

The captain nodded his head, knowing he could not lie after going through reeducation.

"Who are you?" he asked Commander Aggo 1.

"I am Lieutenant Globo 27, the acting captain of this ship," he answered the captain with a straight face. "I was the only one left with any knowledge of command."

Nodding his head, he asked what had happened.

Acting Captain Globo 27 motioned for Reaol 10 to give the explanation.

"We caught up with the traitors hiding on the moon of a desolate world, and he was killed in the fight that followed. We have a complete report written up and will file it once we land." He looked at the captain with a blank expression on his face. "Our computer is down."

"Very well. See that you do," he said, glaring at Hunter. "Did you capture any of them?"

"No sir. They were all killed during the action resisting." Reaol 10 said with the same blank look on his face.

"I see," he said with a half grin on his face.

"Very well. You are cleared to land. Be sure to file that report once you land." He turned to leave.

After the boarding crew had left, Captain Savoy looked at Hunter and said, as he wiped his brow, "That was close. Be sure to write up a report and file it after we land. I would not put it past him to check."

"Yes sir," Hunter said, looking at him, "Wouldn't Christy do a better job of writing the report than me? She is better at telling stories than I am."

"Probably. But I want you to sign it or it will look suspicious to him. He said he knew you." The Captain looked seriously at him.

"Yes sir. I see what you mean. I will see to it right away." He turned and motioned for Christy to follow him.

"You heard the commander." He smiled at Christy. "Do you have a good report we can write?"

"I think so," she said, looking at him. "But I will need your help writing it."

They went into the galley to work on the report, only to return to the commander a few minutes later. "Sir, the computers are down."

Nash noticed a scout ship following us as we began our descent toward the planet. Entering the atmosphere, while still watching the ship on radar, he said, "The scout ship is returning to the station, sir."

Sitting in our acceleration seats, we began our two-hour descent. As we were descending, we discussed how we would combat MAMI, knowing we had to think of something quickly.

When we had landed we were boarded by a very nice and well-endowed young officer dressed in a uniform, which left very little to the imagination, by the name of Lieutenant Distain 8. She had a scowl on her pretty face as she was coming up the ramp. I wondered what had caused such a nice, shapely young woman to look so angry—and I wondered how much trouble we were in.

As she came closer, I grew more and more concerned. She had

three strong, heavily armed men with her.

Stopping in front of Captain Savoy, she said with authority, "You and four others will come with me. You . . . you . . . you . . . and you— pointing at Christy, Abbrelle, Hunter, and me. She turned and went back down the ramp. The captain led the way down the ramp and we fell in step behind him.

One man was waiting at the bottom of the ramp and the remaining two followed behind us.

CHAPTER 9

Walking away from the ramp, we noticed all the activity that was being carried out around the base. There were combat vehicles of all types being loaded for transportation on a large transport ship accompanied by their personnel.

"Where are they headed for?" asked Commander Aggo 1.

"They are being deployed elsewhere," was the curt reply from the lieutenant.

"Oh." The commander looked very concerned, but shrugged his shoulders as he continued following her.

We crossed the hot and steamy tarmac just as the rain ended a few minutes earlier. We watched all of the activity that was being carried everywhere we looked. The base seemed very busy indeed.

The main administration building was surrounded by many men and women, both military and civilian, hurriedly going about their seemingly important business. We were stopped and questioned as to what our business at the building was by several guards standing at the entrance of the building.

Upon recognizing Lieutenant Distain 8, we were immediately allowed to pass. We were told to report to Major Calm 27 and were dispatched a guards to accompany us to the Lift. The Major was on the second floor. We thanked the sergeant and followed her into the building.

"Distain 8 . . . I knew someone by that name a long time ago," Hunter said, looking very thoughtful, walking faster to catch up to her. "But she was just a little . . . just a young girl.

She glanced at him as they walked side by side. She said very quietly to him, "Hi, Reaol 10. The last I heard you had been sent to reeducation." She smiled up at him. Looking at the rest of us, quickly dropping the smile, she stopped at the Lift doors asking, "Who is he?" She pointed at me. She then looked at Abbrelle and Christy, nodded to each of them, and said, "Hi." Turning back to Reaol and glancing at me, "You know civilians are not allowed on this part of the base."

"Let us just say he is military for now. He is a very good and important friend," said Hunter, smiling at her. "You have changed. I did not recognize you."

Lieutenant Distain 8, who I had instantly started to think of as Lisa, gave him an inquiring look, then said, "Come with me."

Once we entered the Lift, she turned to the two men and told one of them to remain here and to let no one use this Lift. She pressed the button for the second floor as she told the second man to come with us.

The door quickly and quietly slid shut behind us and we started to ascend. All of a sudden, the power was quickly cut off and the Lift stopped.

"Listen," she quickly said. "We will not have much time. Do not ask now."—Her hand cutting off any questions—"I am with Victor, as is this man, so is the major we are about to meet. Do not ask any questions now," she finished saying as the power was restored and the Lift resumed its ascent.

When the door opened, we stepped out into the control tower and were met by yet another guard.

He immediately said, "Follow me." He turned and started walking toward a group of officers standing and talking on the far side of the large, well-lit room. Walking up to them he quickly saluted and said calmly, "Major Calm 27, sir, Lieutenant Distain 8 is here, sir."

"Thank you Sergeant." Then turning to the group of officers, he said, "Gentlemen, if you will excuse me." He looked at us. "Please come with me."He walked toward an office. Opening the door, he motioned us to enter.

Lieutenant Distain 8, reaching into a pocket, which the uniform did not appear to have room for, pulled out a small White Noise Device and activated it.

"Now then," the major said, looking at us. He turned to Commander Aggo 1 and held out his hand, saying I am Major Calm 27, and of course you know Lieutenant Distain 8." She stood in the room with a smile on her face.

Commander Aggo 1 turned to Distain 8. "Yes, how are you my dear? I did not recognize you at first. It has been so long. The last time I saw you, you were still in school, and you have grown into a . . . lovely woman." Commander Aggo 1 placed a hand on her shoulder and pulled her into a tight embrace.

"I . . . Uh . . .am fine, unc—sir."

"Uncle in private my dear," he said holding her tightly again.

"Sir, there will be time for that later," the major said. "We can only leave the Device on for a short time. Why are you here and what can we do for you? Sir, so you know, I am her stepfather."

"Yes," he replied, looking at Distain 8. "I heard your mother had remarried. After . . . " Getting back to business, he said, "Please call me Captain Savoy when talking about us to others. I will explain later."

"Yes sir," The major said.

"This will be Hunter, Christy, Abbrelle," he said, pointing at each of them.

"And this is Steve." He pointed to me. "He, I hope, has the answers to our problems."

The Major looked at me, and then questioningly back at the Commander.

"I hope you are right. We have started deploying the troops."

"In that case, I hope I am to. I have to assume the repentance movement has grown?" Captain Savoy asked the Major.

"Yes sir, it has. But for now we had better get on with this meeting before someone becomes suspicious," he said, nodding at the box, asking why we had came here.

"One moment," I said, holding up a hand. "May we call the lieutenant Lisa?" I looked at her well-developed body as she stood. "And perhaps you, George?"

"Why?" the Major asked, looking at me questioningly.

"I will explain later," said Captain Savoy. "But I think it may be a very good suggestion. For now I think it may be safer if we referred to each other by these names." He motioned for Lisa to turn off the White Noise Device.

As Lisa was placing the Device back into her unseen pocket, the door opened and a captain walked in with three well-armed men, demanding to know what was going on.

"What is going on? Why are you in here?" he yelled, looking around at us as we stood staring at him.

"What is the meaning of this Captain!" demanded Major Calm 27. "I was just about to get a report from these people when you came barging in and rudely interrupted us."

"Sorry sir, I was informed that the *SS 927-C* had just landed here. They were sent to chase the traitor Commander Aggo 1 and left toward the other side of the galaxy. What are they doing back in this side of the galaxy? And where s the traitor?"

"That is what I heard too, Captain," he quickly answered. "If you had not interrupted, I would have had the answer by now." He turned toward Captain Savoy who quickly spoke up and said that Reaol 10 had been working on that report. "But the computers on the ship broke down," he continued, "and he has not been able to file it yet. We were hoping we could file it here. May use a computer, Major sir?"

"You," the captain all but screamed at Hunter, "will have the report for me in one hour. In triplicate! Is that understood!"

The major, turning to look at the fuming captain, said with a stern look on his face, "You are overstepping your authority, Captain. He will file the report when I have finished with this interrogation, *in triplicate*. Is that clear Captain!"

The captain, looking at him angrily, merely said, "Yes sir."

"If you wish you may stay while Lieutenant Reaol 10 gives his verbal report," the Major said to the captain. Turning to Hunter he said. "Proceed."

Reaol 10 then proceeded to tell our side of what happened—how the commander had been confronted on one planet but managed to escape, having flown into a heavy atmospheric storm, then having been caught on the moon of another planet where their ship had been attacked, suffering heavy losses when they fought back, and losing several of the crew in the fight. Finally, he told how their captain and all of the crew had been killed when they refused to surrender. The remaining crew had to work doubly hard, since they were short–handed, to return. And that is why the remaining crew returned from the other side of the galaxy.

"A very interesting story," said the captain. "Have it on my desk in one hour, in triplicate." He marched out with his men following closely behind him.

"You may use the computer in this office," said Major Calm 27.

"Will you help me Christy? You are a better at typing than I am."

"I will help you," said Lieutenant Distain 8, giving Hunter a very *interesting* look.

"Yes, why don't you." Christy stepped away from the desk.

Lisa sat down at the computer and brought up the proper form. She started typing what Hunter told her, as he looked over her shoulder, watching her . . . typing.

"I think someone finds someone else interesting," said Abbrelle, looking at them and stepping closer to me.

Charles Aldrich

CHAPTER 10

Melvick came striding purposely up the long hallway, his heels making a load clicking noise on the marble flooring.

He pushed open the door marked "Chancellor—Private" without stopping, showing no sign of respect for the office or the man. As he pushed the door open, he knocked the secretary down who was standing at the file cabinet near the door, with his arrogant entry.

Not saying a word of apology, he looked down at the secretary and scowled. She slowly got to her feet and gave him an inquisitive look as she picked up the papers she had dropped—her breasts firm enough that they did not move as she did.

"Is the chancellor in?" he asked, as he reached for the door handle of his office.

"I'll check. Who should I say is calling?" asked Miss Chan 3, the secretary, looking at him sternly.

Melvick looked back at her just as sternly. "Never mind, I'll see for myself." He reached for the door handle.

"You can't go in there," she yelled. She leaped from the file cabinet she was standing next to and tried to stop him from opening the door.

Melvick threw open the door, brushing her aside, running his hand over her chest as he did. He walked undisturbed into the room, with Miss Chan 3 following closely on his heels stammering that he could not go in there.

"I'm sorry sir. He just barged in," she said, looking at the chancellor.

Looking up from the letter he had just finished, ready to discipline the intruder, he saw who had been so audacious as to barge into his office without being announced. Seeing that it was Melvick, he said to his secretary, "It's alright Miss Chan 3. I'll take care of it." He gave her a half apologetic look. "That will be all for now."

"What do you want?" he asked coldly, looking at Melvick, fury showing in his eyes and voice.

"Now, now—is that any way to talk after all we have done for you?" Melvick stared at him.

"If I had known what it was going to cost me, I would not have agreed to this when you approached me last Cycle."

"Ah, but you did know, didn't you?" he said to him.

"Yes, to my shame, I did," said Chancellor Aggo 2.

"Let's forget that for now," said Melvick, smiling at him. "We need to decide what we will do with Commander Aggo 1 and his crew who may have just landed at Starbase Outreach. They can cause us a lot of trouble. It also looks as if Reaol 10 has overcome his *reeducation* and has returned to the commander. I thought he gave in too easy." Melvick looked distantly out the window, but with a thoughtful look on his face.

"I did not think my father would object so strongly to your ideas," said the chancellor, rubbing his hand over his face. "Is there anything we can do?"

"Do? . . . Do? Why of course there is something we can do! We will continue with our plans. It will take more than one man to stop us." Melvick now glared at the chancellor. "Now get on the phone and order that he be found and brought in immediately."

As the Chancellor picked up the phone, he wondered if he really should order that his father be brought in. Questioning for the first time whether he was doing the right thing for his world. Looking at the phone, he almost set it down. But as he looked over at Melvick, he knew he was in too deep to change his mind now. He would have to comply with the order. There was no mistaking Melvick's tone. It had been an order.

Still a little unsure, he called the Commander of the Armed Forces and told him to come to his office.

"Why did you do that?" Melvick demanded of him. "You know he is not one of us."

"I . . . forgot," he said, not really having forgotten. "I will think of something, but you had better leave before he gets here."

"Yes, I suppose I should. It would not do for him to see me here," Melvick said, still scowling. "Just don't mess this up. We all have too much at stake here."

"Yes." The chancellor looked thoughtful. "I suppose you had better leave. I don't want you to be seen here."

"What are you going to do about your secretary? She saw me come in. She is new, isn't she?"

"Yes, I'll think of something."

"Where is your regular secretary, Mrs. Wilde 4?"

"She's out sick. It will be alright. This one is a temporary secretary, her second day here. She does not know who you are." Chancellor Aggo 2 looked distantly at him.

"I hope you are right. We cannot afford to mess this up." Melvick pulled open the door and stormed out of the office. He didn't even glance at Miss Chan 3 standing by the file cabinet, busily filing where he had caused her drop on the floor earlier.

As Melvick threw open the door and stormed out, Aggo 2 stepped into the room and said, "Miss Chan 3, will you please come into my office."

"Yes sir." She laid the unfinished filing on top of the cabinet and followed him into his office.

Get your steno pad and sit over there and take notes on what is said. Then prepare orders from the notes after the Commander of the Armed Forces leaves."

"Yes sir." She quickly left the room to get her steno pad.

They only had to wait about five minutes when the commander knocked at the door.

When he entered, he saw Miss Chan 3 sitting in a chair, her shapely legs crossed under her short skirt, and her firm breasts between her arms, ready to take notes. He looked questioningly at the chancellor. "Yes sir, what is it?"

The chancellor explained what he wanted him to do as Miss Chan 3 sat taking notes, preparing to write up the orders the chancellor was giving to the commander. The chancellor then dictated how he wanted Aggo 1 captured and returned to the capital as soon as possible.

"You will act upon these orders as soon as they are delivered to you, but not until then. Is that understood?"

"Yes sir," Commander Beck 5 said as he rose. He then turned and left the office.

When he had closed the door after him, the chancellor turned to his secretary and said, "Miss Chan 3, you will type up these notes and make two copies. You will then place one copy in the file for Mrs. Wilde 4 to type up as orders when she returns the first of the Short Cycle. When you have finished this, you will gather your personal belongings and go home, taking the other copy of these notes and hand deliver them to Major Calm 27 at his office at Starbase Outreach. You will then leave for an extended vacation, telling no one but Major Calm 27 where you will be, and be sure to tell no one what the notes say except Major Calm 27. You may have to do some . . . things you do not agree with. Can you do that?"

"Um . . . I believe so, sir. What kind of things?"

"Have you ever . . . with a man?" he asked, looking questioningly at her.

"Um . . . no sir," she answered.

"Well, you may have to. You're not married, are you?"

"Um . . . no sir."

"Well, you may be after this mission."

"Yes sir." She looked totally perplexed. "But I don't completely understand."

"That's alright Miss Chan 3. Just do as I asked and tell no one but Major Calm 27 what you are doing or where you will be when you leave him. He will help you with all of the arrangements." Still not understanding, she just looked at him.

When she had finished typing the notes, she collected her belongings and went into the chancellor's office and told him she was done and ready to leave as he had instructed.

"Fine. Remember, tell no one until you have delivered this to Major Calm 27 personally. Here is some money, and give him this note." He reached into a drawer and pulled out a large quantity of money and handed it to her. "Take a commercial flight and do not to let anyone know where you are going or why." He gave her enough money to make the trip and more, telling her that the extra was for the trip. "And be careful. Now hurry and make the arrangements."

"But sir, it is only mid Wake Period and people will wonder why I am leaving."

"Just tell them I gave you the rest of the day off so you can go and make arrangements with your . . . fiancé . . . for your wedding. Yes that will work. Now go, and please be careful."

"Yes sir. But I have no fiancé," she said as she reached for the door, looking back over her shoulder at him.

"That's OK. Just say he has just returned from a space mission and was not sure when you would arrive. Major Calm 27 will know what to do. Or would you rather say you're his mistress?"

"But . . . " she started to say.

"Oh, just make up a story then. But say you are to be married," said the chancellor, exasperated.

I MEET Abbrelle

Later, as she boarded the plane for her flight and found her seat she said to herself, "I wonder what this is all about? What have I gotten myself into now?"

CHAPTER 11

When Miss Chan 3 landed at the airport, she quickly walked off the plane and out of the terminal. She spoke with a security guard at the door and told him she wanted to go to the Starbase Outreach, but that she suspected that a man was following her. She asked if the security guard would please detain him. She then hailed a taxi.

Getting into the first cab she said to the driver, "Take me to the Starbase. I am going there to meet my—fiancé." She settled into the well-worn seat.

"Congratulations," he said, smiling at her reflection in the mirror. "You know you will not be allowed on the base without authorization, don't you."

"No, I did not know that. He didn't tell me," she replied, looking surprised.

"All you will have to do is ask see the base commander and tell him who your fiancé is and that you are there to marry him. I'm sure he will help you." The driver was still looking in the mirror at her. "I'm sure he will tell your fiancé you are there. He is a very lucky man," he said.

When they pulled up to the main gate of the Starbase, a guard came over to the taxi and asked, "May I help you?"

"Yes," the driver said. "This young lady needs to see the base commander. She is to be married."

"Well miss, the taxi is not allowed on base. If you will please wait over here on this bench, I will call the commander's office and have him send a car for you. Does he know you are coming?" he asked, as she slowly got out of the taxi, her skirt riding up high.

"Um, no . . . um, I mean I'm not sure," she said to the guard while the taxi drove away while she was trying to inch her skirt down.

"Well, sit here and I will call the commander's office and find out if he will see you." The guard watched her as she sat down on the bench, her skirt riding well up above mid–thigh. She looked perplexed, holding her purse tightly to her bare chest.

Walking back into the guard shack, shaking his head, the guard called the lieutenant in charge.

Lieutenant Distain 8 knocked on the commander's door. After he responded she opened the door and said, "Sir, the main gate just called and said there is a young lady that needs to talk to you about getting married to someone here on the base."

Instantly recognizing the code words "to get married" he looked up at her and asked, "Did she say who she was to marry?" hoping to get more information.

"No sir. All she would only say is that he did not know when she would arrive and that she was to get in touch with you and that you would notify him when she arrived."

The lieutenant, clearly confused, stared at the commander sitting at his desk, rubbing his chin. "You don't suppose?" he said quietly. Finally, he looked up. "Very well, call my driver, Sergeant Coup 3. You go with him to pick her up. Find out what you can."

She looked at him strangely and finally said, "Yes sir. Is there anything particular I am to look for?"

"No," he replied.

She turned and left the room.

After she had left, the commander reached in to his desk and took out a small, silver box and plugged it to a switch under his desk, then placed it on a hidden shelf, special-made for it, under his desk.

When the commander's car pulled up to the guard post, the sergeant came out of the building and said, "They are here for you . . . Miss." He looked at Miss Chan 3 sitting still, clutching her purse tightly to her chest—and that leg . . . she was showing.

Standing up, still tightly clutching her purse, she followed the sergeant to the car.

As soon as Lieutenant Distain 8 got out of the car, the sergeant snapped to attention and saluted. "Here she is Ma'am."

"Very well Sergeant. I'll take it from here." She returned his salute.

The lieutenant turned to Miss Chan 3. "Now Miss, you say you are here to marry someone, but he does not know when you will get here. Is that right?" She looked suspiciously at her.

"That's right. He doesn't know I am here yet. I was told to say that and to talk to only Major Calm 27."

Turning to her driver, she said, "Sergeant, will you please search her?"

"Yes Ma'am." He started toward her.

"Ww . . . what?" she stammered, holding up a hand. "You can see all I have on is my skirt and shoes.

"What's in the purse?" he asked as he pulled out a security wand and swiped it over her and the purse she was still holding tightly to her chest, raising her skirt slightly as he did so.

"Nothing, just the usual." She glared at him. If you raise my skirt any more, you will see *everything.*

"All clear," he said to the lieutenant as he put the security wand away again.

"I see," said the lieutenant. "Please step into the car Miss . . .?"

"Chan 3," she shot back with a somewhat nervous look.

While they drove to the headquarters building, Lieutenant Distain 8 was constantly asking her questions, to which the only reply she received was that Chan 3 was only to talk to Major Calm 27. Finally giving up, they rode the rest of the way in silence. When they pulled up in front of the headquarters building, they got out and Lieutenant Distain 8 motioned for Miss Chan 3 to precede her as they walked into Lieutenant Distain 8's office. The lieutenant then told the driver to wait in her office with Miss Chan 3 while she spoke to the major.

Lieutenant Distain 8 spoke to Major Calm 27, letting him know she had returned with the young lady. She advised him of what little she had found out. She then returned to her office and told Miss Chan 3 and the driver both to come with her.

When they entered his office the major stood up and said very causally, "I understand you are here to get married, Miss . . . ?" motioning for both his driver and the Lieutenant to come in and close the door. "Would you please tell me who the lucky man is so we may tell him his lovely bride is here?"

"Miss Chan 3," she replied looking at the major as she stood before his desk. She held out the package of papers as he continued to stare at her. "All I know is what is here in these papers."

"Did you read them?" he asked as he reached for them. She started to draw them back, first looking at the lieutenant and then the sergeant, both staring at her.

"Yes sir. I took the dictation and had to type them up. So I guess you could say I read them." She finally handed them to him.

After reading the papers he reached down and turned the White Noise Device on. "Are these to go in to effect immediately?" he asked her.

"No sir. I think the chancellor wanted you to see them first. They won't be put out as orders until the first of the Short Cycle, when Mrs. Wilde 4 types them up. So," she said, "they will not go out until the middle of the Short Cycle when they will be sent by courier to the judge advocate. So it may be as many as two Short Cycles before they will be sent out."

"What exactly were you told to do Miss Chan 3?" he asked, looking up at her as if seeing her for the first time.

She looked around and finally said, "I was told to tell anyone who asked that I was coming here to meet my fiancé and get married. Then I was to say we were leaving on our honeymoon and to tell only you where we were going and that you would make the arrangements."

"I see," said the commander thoughtfully while still looking at her. "Well then, I guess we will have to have a wedding and let you leave on your honeymoon. Do you have a groom in mind?"

"Um—no. I did not know I would need one. I didn't like the idea of being a mistress."

"Lieutenant, take her to your office. I have a few calls to make. I need to find the groom." He gave her a wink and smiled. "I think Reaol 10 would make the perfect groom. Don't you?"

"Yes sir," Lieutenant Distain 8 said, smiling back at him and nodding her head. She took Miss Chan 3 by the arm and escorted her out to her office.

"But . . . but," stammered Miss Chan 3 as they walked out. "I don't really want to get married. Besides, I want to choose my own husband."

After they left, the major reached under his desk and shut off the White Noise Device.

Leading Miss Chan 3 into her office, she placed a finger to her lips and mouthed the word *bugs* then *bathroom*—she then pointed down the hallway to the restroom.

Nodding her head in understanding, Miss Chan 3 quickly asked, "May I go to the restroom? Would you please show me where it is?"

"Yes, follow me," Lieutenant Distain 8 said as she lead Miss Chan 3 out of her office and headed with her to the restroom.

Once in the restroom, the lieutenant went quickly to the sink and turned the water on full force. "Now we can talk quietly," she said. She quickly explained the major's plan to the best of her knowledge.

"But I don't even know this Reaol 10."

"I do," she said. "He can and will keep you safe from almost anyone or anything. He is good-looking too, with a strong, nice body, and a nice . . . It will just be a sham wedding." She looked at Miss Chan 3 and said, "Make an excuse for the water." She reached down and turned it off.

Quickly Miss Chan 3 said, "I never was able to use a restroom when others are present without running the water so they can't . . . hear me." She smiled at Lieutenant Distain 8.

Giving her an OK sign, the water, they walked out of the restroom and returned to the office.

They giggled as they walked back to the lieutenant's office, discussing her upcoming *wedding* as they went. While they sitting in her office, still discussing the wedding, the intercom buzzed: "Lieutenant, would you and Miss Chan 3 please come in here?"

"Yes Major," she said, quickly getting up and leading Miss Chan 3 back into the commander's office.

"Have a seat, Miss Chan 3," he said after they walked in.

"I have talked to the groom and he will be here shortly. But first we have some paperwork to complete." He noticed that her skirt had ridden up quite high, showing her legs.

"I see your parents have gone with the new trend of giving you a first name, Linda. Is that right?" He indicated with his expression for her to go along with him.

"Yes. That's right. They thought it was cute," she said, clearly not understanding what was going on, but deciding to go along with him as if that was her name.

"Ah—and here I have your fiancé's papers. Let's see. Ah yes. Hunter Reaol 10. Yes, that should do it." He laid the papers down. At the same time, he flipped the White Noise Device switch again and said, "False names mean no marriage."

"But, that . . . " Linda Chan 3 started to say.

He flipped the switch off again. "There, that should do it," he said, making a lot of noise while he finished writing by shuffling papers around—making as much noise as he could. "Now we wait for the groom." He gesturing for them to stay seated. "He should be here shortly."

After a several minutes passed, the major stood up. "He doesn't appear to be coming. I think we should go and meet him, don't you? I'm sure he will be anxious to see you." He looked at her long legs and then at her chest—then at his watch, making a lot of noise as he did.

"Yes sir. I agree," said Lieutenant Distain 8, also making a lot of noise.

Linda, meanwhile, just looked at both of them, as if they were crazy.

The major mouthed, "We need to get out of here."

They walked out of his office and crossed the busy street to the parade ground that was just across from his building. They talked quietly while they walked.

Linda Chan 3 was walking next to Major Calm 27. She looked up to him and asked, "What are we doing?"

"We are going to meet your fiancé." he said as he looked around see if anyone was paying them any attention. Not seeing anyone he continued, "Now that we are out of the office, it should be safe enough to talk. Why did Chancellor Aggo 2 send you here?"

"I don't know. It's like I told you in your office. He had me type the notes I had taken and then he told me to bring a copy to you, and my cover story would be that I was coming here to get married. He said I could be someone's mistress, but I did not like that idea. I could never do that. Then I was supposed to leave on an extended trip. A honeymoon. You were to be the only one to know where I would be."

"You are sure there was not anything else? Maybe something that you are forgetting? Did he talk about anything else?"

"Well—he did talk to Melvick before he called me in. Melvick left before I took the notes though. He did look awful, concerned, as he left," Miss Chan 3 said as they were walking.

"And that was it?" he asked.

"Yes. He gave me the orders about bringing the paperwork to you after Melvick had left. I thought that was strange. Always before he would have told me what to do while someone was still in the office."

The major continued looking around to see if anyone was watching them.

"Why are you looking around so much?" Miss Chan 3 asked. "Are you looking for someone?"

"Yes." He turned his head and looked behind them again. "I am trying to make sure we are not being followed."

"You mean like that man over there?" she asked, nodding with her head at a man that was keeping pace with them on the sidewalk about fifty feet away.

"Could be," he answered, looking at the man. "Do you know him?"

"No," Miss Chan 3 said. "But he has been following me ever since I left the office. I saw him lounging in the hall at the capital when I walked out. Then I saw him again as I was getting my ticket for the plane. Once on the plane he tried to talk and get fresh with me, and then again when I landed at the airport. He said he was traveling here and would give me a ride so that I would not have to get a taxi. He followed me out and it seemed like he was trying to catch me as I got into the cab. And now here he is again."

"Sergeant Coup 3, will you please see if you can talk to him and find out why he was following Miss Chan 3?"

The sergeant nodded and took off as if he had to be somewhere else, heading away from the man in question.

As they continued walking, Miss Linda Chan 3 asked in a concerned voice, "Where are we going?"

"To meet your fiancé," was the only answer she got.

Later, as they continued walking across the parade ground, she saw Sergeant Coup 3 returning, walking up to them from the opposite direction he had left in.

"He saw me coming and took off, sir. I lost him in the commissary."

"Very well Sergeant," he said as they continued to walk.

When they finally reached the BOQ (Bachelor Officers Quarters) they turned left and took a path that led behind the building, following it to a copse of trees that was between the building and the base fence. When they reached a crossroads, he turned and then asked the sergeant if they were being followed.

"Not that I can tell, sir."

"Very well, stay here and keep watch," he told the sergeant.

Major Calm 27 led the rest of the group down the path and crossed the base fence through a hole in the wire. They soon came to a vine-covered building that looked to be deserted and was set back among trees. He knocked several times at the door, stopped, then knocked several more times. The door was quickly answered by a young woman he called Emulate 2.

As she stood at the door, he said, "I have someone here that I'm sure Reaol 10 would to like meet."

Abbrelle looked curiously at the people with the major and at Miss Chan 3. She then nodded her head, stepped to one side, and allowed them to enter.

Miss Chan 3 noticed as they entered that there was a very well-built and handsome young man about her age—maybe a little older—standing to one side of the door with a weapon trained on them.

"It's OK Hunter," Abbrelle said to him as she closed the door.

"Hunter!" exclaimed Miss Chan 3. "Are you supposed to be my fiancé?" she asked inquisitively, yet smiling slightly at him at the same time. She stared at him with wide eyes, taking in all of his six foot three inches well-built frame, with his broad shoulders and thin waist. He was holding his weapon, pointing it at them.

Lieutenant Distain 8 looked at him with a big grin on her face. She said, "That's right, Linda. This is Hunter Reaol 10, your new fiancé."

"Well, if I *have* to get married, at least it's to a good-looking man." She was still looking him over, almost regretting the marriage would not be for real.

"Wh—what's this about?" asked Reaol 10." He looked back and forth between Miss Chan 3 and Major Calm 27.

"This is Miss Linda Chan 3, and Lieutenant Distain 8 is right. She is going to be your new bride," replied Major Calm 27, smiling at Hunter. He then went on to explain how Miss Linda Chan 3 had brought a note from Chancellor Aggo 2 stating that Commander Aggo 1 was to be apprehended and sent to the capital for questioning, and how they had to solidify her alibi for being here by having her get married and getting her to safety quickly.

"O . . . K, but how do I fit into this?" Hunter asked, as he looked at Linda with renewed interest, liking what he saw. He smiled at her.

"Well we thought you could act as her new husband and bodyguard and keep her safe" replied Major Calm 27.

"I . . . we . . . thought you could have a fake marriage ceremony and then you could take her to a south sea island and act as her husband until this is all over," said Lieutenant Distain 8, looking at Hunter but glancing and smiling quickly at Linda.

"I will be no man's mistress," Linda said.

"Things are starting to speed up fast and I don't think it will be long before we will be able to expose Melvick for the traitor that he is." The major continued looking at Hunter, but glanced at Linda and smiled.

Hunter rubbed his face, casting his eyes toward the ceiling and then bringing them back to the major and Lieutenant Distain 8—Lisa—with a forlorn and puzzled look on his face. Tearing his eyes away from Linda, he asked, "Who's idea was it to have her marry me?"

"Mine," Lieutenant Distain 8 quickly said with a large smile on her face. "I . . . we," she quickly amended, looking at Major Calm 27 and pointing at him over her shoulder, "thought you would make the perfect husband. . .MMM. . . bodyguard for her." She looked at him through downcast eyes. Then she raised her head and looked at Linda, still with a big smile on her lips. "Besides, you will make the perfect bodyguard and husband for her," she said brightly as she smiled up at him.

"Come on," Lisa Distain 8 said, grabbing his arm. "Let's go in and make plans for the big wedding." Still smiling, she dragged him into the next room, ignoring Major Calm 27 as she went. "We have a lot to discuss. Your wedding is tomorrow." Linda following them closely behind with a confused look her face.

After we all sat down at the table, which included Commander Aggo 1 and me, we discussed all that occurred since I had gotten involved with this group. We started discussing everything but the wedding—everyone talking among themselves.

After discussing the plan he had came up, with a few minor changes suggested by Commander Aggo 1, Major Calm 27 stood up.

Hunter then reluctantly asked in a quiet voice, "How are we going to handle this . . . wedding?"

Lisa looked at him and broke into laughter. "Simple," she said, looking up at him. "You just go in front of the chaplain tomorrow and say 'I Do' and he will pronounce you married. Simple." She looked over at Linda and they both started laughing. "I am making all the arrangements," Lisa said as she looked over at him.

Then Lisa took Linda's arm and they both walked out the door and stood outside, smiling and laughing, talking among themselves, waiting for Major Calm 27.

"That's not what I meant," Hunter mumbled, looking distraught after as they walked out.

The wedding the next day was a small affair, held in the chaplain's office instead of the chapel. It was witnessed by a lieutenant from

Melvick's personal guard, who had followed Linda, but was unknown to the rest of them. The insignia on his collar, however, indicated he was a member of the MAMI, who had come to check on Miss Chan 3 to make sure her story for coming to Starbase Outreach to be married was indeed valid.

"I don't know how they found out so fast," said Lisa to Linda.

"They must have heard me telling the other secretary that I was coming here to get married," Linda replied quietly.

After the wedding the chaplain said to Hunter and Linda, "Will you please sign these papers?" He handed Hunter a pen and indicated where to sign.

"What papers?" they both asked, startled as they looked at him.

"The marriage papers." the chaplain said, glancing at the lieutenant who was still standing in the back of the room watching and listening.

"You have to sign them so I can file them with the ministry. Otherwise, your marriage will not be official. Will your witnesses please sign too?" he asked after Linda and Hunter had signed the papers. "I know it is easy to overlook these small things, but . . . "

He turned around and said softly so only they could hear as they stood beside his desk, "We are going to have to make this official since that lieutenant is here."

"You mean I am married to Hunter for real?" exclaimed the now Linda Chan-Reaol, just as quietly to the chaplain so as not to be heard by the lieutenant either. She glanced at him as he stood watching them.

"I'm afraid so." The chaplain handed her the marriage license. "We have to make it official since I am sure he will be checking with the ministry. You can always get it annulled if you don't . . . Ahhh, in which case you can . . . "

"Well," said Hunter, looking at Linda as she stood holding the large bouquet of flowers that she had carried throughout the ceremony up against her barely covered chest. She looked up at him apprehensively.

"I suppose we will have to make the best of it for now." He leaned down and gave her a long, passionate kiss on the lips. "But rest assured that I will not try in any way to take advantage of you," he said quietly to her as he leaned down and kissed her again. "Although . . ." Standing back up, he reached out for her hand and asked very calmly, "Shall we leave now, my darling wife?"

When they exited the chapel doors, they were met with a shower of birdseed, thrown by the few well-wishers who were waiting for them.

As they were climbing into the car to leave, the lieutenant from MAMI leaned close to Hunter and said with a sneer to his voice, "Nice bod. Where are you headed?"

"Somewhere quiet and private," Hunter answered, shoving the Lieutenant back. He slid in next to Linda and slammed the door in the lieutenant's face and drove away.

CHAPTER 12

"Come," said Major Calm 27. "Let's retire to the park where we will have the reception. You did make the arrangements didn't you, Lieutenant Distain 8?"

"Yes sir. All the arrangements have been made and are now being carried out. I also told the driver where we were holding the reception. They should be there any second."

"Very good." He nodded his head to her and held out his hand. "Shall we go?"

When they arrived at the park, which was several miles away from the chapel, they found Hunter and Linda already there talking to Commander Aggo1 with Christy and Abbrelle standing off to one side talking to me. We had not been able to go to the wedding since we were afraid we would be recognized. None of us were in a very good mood, not being able to attend the wedding—even if it was a sham wedding. But having found out who had been there made us understand why we could not.

"What is wrong?" asked Major Calm 27 as he got out of his car and walked up to us.

"We were just discussing why they had to file the marriage papers," replied Commander Aggo 1.

"They had to file the papers to make it official," said Lieutenant Distain 8, walking up to them in her full-length, semi–shear, topless dress, with Major Calm 27. Holding on to the major's arm, she said, "There was a lieutenant there from MAMI who came just after the start of the ceremony and stayed until the papers were signed and they had left," pointing to Hunter and Linda. "We had no choice but to file the papers."

"I suppose it won't matter," said Commander Aggo 1.

"Won't matter? Won't matter!" screamed Linda Chan-Reaol, having heard what they were talking about. She came over to them, swinging her arms, causing her breasts to move in the most *interesting* way. "I had no intentions of getting married!" she screamed, pointing to Hunter.

"Take it easy." Commander Aggo turned to Linda and tried to calm her down. "We will get this all straightened out and get the marriage annulled."

"Annulled? But that is against my religion," she said, starting to calm down, now realizing what she had said and how it would affect her life.

"Well then, you know, things may work out better this way. Now you won't be traveling as an unmarried couple. Besides, give him a chance. You may like being married to him," said Abbrelle. "I know he is a pain, but he is an OK brother, and he is good in . . . Besides, he will protect you with his life," she said, looking at Linda.

"But being forced into a marriage? That is why . . ." she said before she became quiet with a thoughtful look on her face. "There is that," said Linda Chan-Reaol, trying to cover up her slip. "What name will I go by now?"

"You could always go by Mrs. Linda Reaol 10," said Hunter, coming up to her and putting his arms around her waist, holding her tight as he gazed into her eyes. She looked up into his, not trying to get out of his arms but laying her head back against his broad chest and pulling his arms tighter up under her . . . .

"I suppose I could," she said as she felt a slight shiver of thrill slide through her from his touch. "But I think I will use the new way and go by Chan-Reaol. Now I can. . . I have always wanted to but was told to wait until I was married, and then I could. . . .if my husband agreed."

"Yes—well, whatever," said Major Calm 27. "I think we should get down to business and discuss what we are going to do about MAMI's attempts to capture you, Walt, and their plan to take over our world."

"Yes," Commander Walt Aggo1 said, looking back at Major Calm 27.

"Steve do you have any ideas on this matter?" Major Calm 27 asked, looking at me.

"Well, what do you know about this movement?" I asked them both as I walked over to them.

A long discussion ensued on everything that was known about the movement and what the MAMI were planning on doing.

While we talked, Abbrelle, Christy, and Lisa brought over plates of some very good, but strange looking food that had been prepared for the party. They handed a plate to each of us.

"Is here anything we can do to help?" Abbrelle asked as the women walked up to us. "Will you . . . pointing to the dab of frosting that was on her . . . chest."

"Well, can you turn invisible and sneak in to their headquarters?" I asked, partly kidding—after I had . . . the frosting.

"Well, you know we have some control over certain things in a person's mind," said Christy. "But I can't turn invisible."

"Me either," said Abbrelle. She stopped beside Christy and looked at me. "Why?"

"Just wishful thinking on my part." I looked at them standing in their topless dresses they had worn for the party and then smiled at both of them.

"Yes!" I remembered the way Christy had made me see clothes on her that were not really there when we first met. She had also made me see changes to her looks. Their dresses started to shimmer the more I thought about what she had told me, then completely disappeared.

Looking at me, the major said, "Those were nice dresses, were they not?" We both stood looking at the four women, now standing there . . .

"That might work," I said mostly to myself. I had a faraway look on my face as I thought more about it. All remnants of their dresses were completely gone now.

"What might work?" Christy and Abbrelle both asked at the same time.

"That just may work," I repeated again to myself. I then started to explain the basics of my plan to everyone.

"Yes." They all agreed when I was done explaining the basic outline of my plan.

"The only problem will be getting into their headquarters. It would be better if we could be invisible and just walk in—or had someone on the inside who was invisible. I don't suppose any of you know where it is, do you?" I asked, looking at them.

"I know," said Hunter, having joined us earlier when I had been explaining the plan to everyone. "I may even have a way to get in," he said, looking at us as he held Linda closely to his side. Her dress had disappeared too, leaving her standing. . . . "The only thing is that it will require the help of Linda." He looked down at her. "It could be dangerous if it doesn't work."

"Will it be more dangerous than bringing you the information was?" she asked, looking up at him with a strange look on her face that said she would do almost anything for him and then at Commander Aggo 1.

"I hope not, but it might be," Hunter said, still gazing down into her upturned face—her dress completely gone now.

"If it is one of your plans," said Abbrelle looking at Hunter. "It probably will be."

Jerking his eyes away from Linda he said, "Not if I can help it, it won't be."

"Well, let's hear it," said Commander Walt Aggo 1. "I am open to almost anything at this point," he added, looking at Hunter and Linda, Abbrelle, Lisa, and Christy, able to see through the "glimmer" as they all stood there in the park.

Hunter explained his plan to get them into the MAMI headquarters.

All of our eyes grew wide and several of us shook our heads the further he went with his plan.

"And you don't think that it will not be dangerous?" asked Abbrelle when he had finished telling us his plan.

"Not any more than your part will be." He went on to explain how it would be up to her, Christy and I to get them out.

"You know plans never seem to work out the way you plan," I said.

"What do you think of it George?" Commander Aggo 1 asked Major Calm 27.

"Well, it could work." He rubbed his chin as he thought it through. "It just might work at that. I am just not sure about Miss Chan 3 going in there though." He looked at her. "A lot will depend on what that lieutenant had to report back on the wedding. If he bought it that you two really were engaged before you had that retraining you had to go through, Hunter, it just might work. You know, "he said unexpectedly, "it is easier to use these new names."

"What would we have to do to make them think Hunter had asked me before he went through the retraining?" she asked, looking at Major Calm 27.

"Well, for one thing you could start wearing traditional married women's clothes and not go topless like unmarried women do. I know you told that lieutenant that you did not because you were never officially engaged. Buuuttt—" He drew out the last word as long as he could.

"But I am not topless, it's see-through. Yes, this is the way young, married women dress now."

"That's right," said Abbrelle, looking sternly at the major. "In fact, many still go topless after the wedding. Men go topless all their lives so why can't women, at least wear see-through tops once they are married.

"Yea." Linda looked at the major as he rubbed his chin again. "You know that a lot of young wives still go without tops now don't you?" she asked, looking at him.

"Yes I know," the major said with a frown. "But I don't agree with it. Well . . .if you were to get pregnant, it would show you were really in love with Hunter and wanted to get married as much as you have claimed you wanted to," he continued.

"Pregnant!" both Linda and Hunter said at the same time.

"But that would mean I would have to . . . And I am still on . . . " Linda started to say, then smiled. "I can always quit taking them."

"Pregnant. But," Hunter said again, "how would that help?"

"Well, it would prove we were really in love and wanted to get married," replied Linda, looking up at him thoughtfully. "What's the matter, don't you want to *try* to get me pregnant? Are you sorry you married me already?" She looked up at him with hurt in her eyes.

"No—no, really, I thought . . . it's just." He looked over at Lisa for help.

"It's no worse than the arranged, loveless, marriage my parents wanted me to go into before I left home," said Linda as she glared up at him with her hands on her hips—finally saying what she had been trying so hard not to say.

"Huh? I thought that arranged marriages went out years ago," Hunter said, looking at Linda, startled.

"Well not in my religion, it hasn't," Linda said with some disgust. "That was why I left home."

"I won't force you into anything. You know our marriage would not have to be permanent if you don't want it to be," Hunter said, somewhat disappointed. "But if you have a child, it will defiantly be permanent."

"Yes, it is permanent. We are officially married and we will stay married if I can help it. But that does not mean we cannot play. . . ." she replied with a glint in her eyes. "I have always wanted to. . . . When I got married, I told myself it would be for life." She looked at Hunter.

"Even if it was arranged."

"Uh oh," Hunter stammered. "Well . . . "

"You don't feel that way?" she asked?

"Well, it will take some getting used to . . . but . . . yes, OK. I'll do it." He looked at her. "Like you just said we can always. . . ."

"And I thought I was the one forced in to this marriage," she said dispassionately.

"I'll try to make sure you never regret this." Hunter sighed as he looked at her, raising her hand to his lips.

"I'm not sure I don't already," she said to herself.

"When do we start this plan?" she asked, looking at the major and commander.

"We will have to wait until after the honeymoon," replied Commander Aggo 1. "That's something you can't fake—unless there is someone else you would rather have for the father."

"No!" Linda exclaimed loudly and fervently. "I'd do it now if we could."

"In front of everyone here?" asked Abbrelle.

"Why not? At least we would have witnesses, and it might be fun, with. . . ." Linda said smiling and looking around.

"You know," I said in her ear as I stood close to her. "Walt and I can both see through the 'glimmer.' "

She put her hands in front of her and started to smile. "Now you tell me." Then she wrapped her arms around me and said, "You naughty man." Then kissed me. "There's your wedding kiss." She stepped back a few feet and held her arms out. "Like what you see?" Then she turned and walked over to Hunter, smiling.

"Being married sure changed her," I said.

"Oh, I don't know," Walt said. "She still looks the same to me."

"It looks like you will get that honeymoon after all," Hunter said to her with a half smile on his lips, as she walked up to him smiling. "What made you so happy all of a sudden?" he asked Linda.

"Maybe I'll tell later." She wrapped her arms around him and gave him a big kiss.

"Well come on," Hunter said. "This is supposed to be a party. Let's have some fun."

CHAPTER 13

Melvick, returning to his office, picked up the phone and called his aide, Lieutenant Blather 3. When he answered he told him to wait outside of Chancellor Aggo 2's office and tell him who came in or who left, then to find out where they went after they left.

When Lieutenant Blather 3 had been watching the office for about an hour Miss Chan 3 came walking out, stuffing some papers into her large purse, as she shut the door and started walking down the hall.

Chatting with other secretaries in the hall, one secretary stopped her and asked if she wanted to join them in having a cup of Kafree (coffee).

Miss Chan 3 explained how she was taking off early so she could go to her apartment and pack for her trip to meet her fiancé and how they were to be married as soon as she got to Starbase Outreach where he was currently stationed.

The other secretary let out a small squeal and wanted to know why she had not let them know so they could have had party for her.

Looking at her a little astonished, Miss Chan 3 explained how he had been gone on a one-year mission and had just returned and wanted to get married now, adding that they had been engaged for a year or more. She said, "I didn't know any of you that well, and it never occurred to me you would want to give me a party."

The other secretary, having made all the appropriate regrets of her having to leave so quickly said, "Well, good luck and congratulations. I have to get going." She waved as she walked away.

The lieutenant followed Miss Chan 3 discreetly to her apartment. He waited outside while calling Melvick and told him what he had found out.

Melvick told him to follow her and make sure she was doing what she claimed she was. "I don't believe her. Follow her all the way to Starbase Outreach, and if you have to, even to the wedding."

He followed her to the airport and stood in line right behind her as she bought her ticket. She then bought a ticket to Starbase Outreach too. While she was sitting in the lounge, he sat next to her and said, "I noticed you bought a ticket to Starbase Outreach. May I ask why you are going there?"

Miss Chan 3 looked up and noticed he was looking more at her breasts than he was at her face. She pointed to her eyes. "My eyes are up here, not down here." She then pointed to her breasts. She explained that she was going there to be married.

He stared at her hard in the eyes. "Pardon me for asking, but I thought girls going to be married usually covered their . . . ah . . . breasts," he asked, looking down at hers again, "after they became engaged?"

"Well some have started waiting until the wedding. We had discussed marrying before he left on this last mission. But that was as far as it got before he had leave. He just called last night and asked me to come to Starbase Outreach and marry him. I'm on my way now to meet him and get married," she answered, looking him in the eye.

"Well, I am going to Starbase Outreach also and I would be very happy to give you a ride out to the base. It would save you the taxi fare. Besides, we could . . . before you are married."

"No thank you, though I do appreciate the offer," she said still smiling at him, turning slightly red. "He told me to take a taxi to the front gate and call Major Calm 27 from there and that I would be picked up."

"He must have high friends there if he told you to call the major." He looked at her with renewed interest. "But I could save you the trouble of having to get a taxi since I am going there anyway. I will have a car waiting for me at the airport." He looked down at her breasts again. "Besides we could . . . ."

"Thank you, but I do not do that," she said. "I'll just take a taxi." She got up and walked to the far side of the waiting lounge, taking a different seat. She saw him looking at her every time she would glance at him.

Upon boarding the plane, she discovered he was seated just across the aisle from her and continually kept staring at her.

He said, looking at her, "I'm sorry. But it's just hard to believe you are getting married in a few days."

"Well I am!" she said forcefully. "So would you please just leave me alone?"

"Yes of course," he said as he closed his eyes, but still looking at her through his partly closed eyes.

When they departed the plane he walked right behind her and asked again if he could give her a lift to the base.

"No thank you!" she said again rather gruffly.

"Well at least let me carry some of that luggage for you," he said as she reached to pick up her bags. Her purse started to slide down her arm. He slipped his arm through the strap of her purse and started to lift it up.

As she grabbed to catch her purse, his hand inadvertently brushed across her right breast.

"Sorry." He drew his hand back across her breast, still holding the strap of her purse, smiling as he did so.

"I've got it." She grabbed her purse away from him, causing his hand to slip across her breast again. She stood up, grabbed her luggage, and she gave him a dark look. "I can handle it myself, thank you." She gave him an icy glare. "I told you I do not . . . before marriage."

"What about after you are married?" he asked, leering at her.

"Not with you."

Clutching her luggage, she turned and stomped away from him heading toward the exit. When she reached the security guard standing next to the exit door, she stopped and looked back and pointed at Lieutenant Blather. She told the guard that he was bothering her and asked if he would please not let him follow her to the taxi. Then she walked out the door as the lieutenant came striding up.

"Sir!" the guard said politely. "Would you please wait here a moment while the lady gets into her taxi?" The guard placed a hand on the lieutenant's chest.

The lieutenant started to push past the guard, but stopped when the guard stepped in front of him and said again quite strongly, "Sir, would you please wait here until after the lady leaves."

Looking angrily at the guard, he stepped back and said, "OK," cursing under his breath and scowling at the guard.

The lieutenant watched as she got in the taxi and drove away. He looked back at the guard. "May I go now?" He pushed the guard's hand off his chest and walked to the official car that was waiting for him next to the curb. The guard watched closely as he left.

◇

Miss Chan 3's taxi pulled up to the main gate at Starbase Outreach. The guard stepped out of the shack and walked over to her. When Miss Chan 3 had gotten out of the taxi and told the guard she wanted to talk to Major Calm 27, the guard asked her to wait. He went back into the guard shack and talked to the officer in charge, who then called the major's office asking for instructions. They would send an aide to pick her up.

Telling his driver to pull to the side of the road, a block short of the gate, Lieutenant Blather 3 waited until the car with Lieutenant Distain 8, Major Calm 27's aide, pulled up. Lieutenant Distain 8 got out in her uniform short skirt and top that stopped just above the top of her large firm breasts and walked over to Miss Chan 3. She started questioning her as to what her business with Major Calm 27 was. After enduring a short, but complete, security check of her, they both got into the car and drove away.

Lieutenant Blather 3, watching the entire scene, quietly said to himself, "I wonder." He turned to his driver. "Driver, take me to the BOQ." "I wonder?" he said again, as he watched the car drive away.

He watched the major and Miss Chan 3 with their escorts walking across the street to the parade grounds, from his room in the BOQ, When they started walking along the parade grounds, he left his room and followed them on the opposite side of the street. He saw a sergeant leave the group and disappear in the commissary.

Saying to himself again, "I wonder." He was still watching three hours later as the group returned from across the parade ground to the major's office. When he learned that the next day there was to be a wedding of Miss Chan 3 and Reaol 10, he picked up his phone and called Melvick, telling him all that had happened.

"Attend the wedding and make sure it is not a fake," Melvick ordered as he slammed the phone back down saying, "Idiot." Melvick thought to himself *What are they up to?* Grabbing his phone, he told his secretary to get him Director Stener.

When Director Stener answered the call, he informed him that he needed a *complete* security and history check ran on Miss Chan 3.

"Yes sir," was the answer he received. "I will have it for you the next Wake Period at the latest."

Placing the phone down, he wondered again what was going on and what they were planning.

The next day, just before mid Wake Cycle, he received a call from Director Stener, who gave him his report on Miss Chan 3. He stated, "She is 21 years old, has had all of the normal childhood ailments, graduated from the local school, leaving home shortly after. I could not find a reason for her leaving since she had always been a very good child. Upon arriving at the capital, and after finishing classes to become a secretary, she obtained a job with the government as a temporary secretary. She had been assigned as a temporary secretary to Chancellor Aggo 2's office when Mrs. Wilde 4 had become ill. She is to be married to Reaol 10 as soon as she reaches Starbase Outreach"—that note having been add just that day.

"Wasn't Reaol 10 just released from the retraining center about 6 months ago?" Melvick asked.

"Yes, I believe he was," said the director said, a thoughtful look crossing his face.

"Check out this Reaol 10 when you finish here," he told Stener. "I want to know where he is and what he is doing."

"Yes sir," he said, then continued. "They are to leave for the Island of Repul for their honeymoon and had booked for a stay of one month." Stener continued reading from the report on his desk. "Reaol 10 is to report back from his leave the day after they return." Stener continued to flip through the papers. "Ah, here it is. It seemed she was to marry an older, but wealthy man, and she objected to the marriage. She and her parents had a big disagreement about her refusing to marry the man since as he was quite a bit older than her. Her parents wanted the marriage because of the money and prestige they would receive. She had left her parents' home. Prior to that," he continued, "she has no record of anything. It seems that she was obedient to her parents and never disobeyed them—never causing any problems at all."

"Did the parents report her disappearance?" asked Melvick in a demanding voice.

"Yes sir. They reported it and were informed when she showed up here in the city and obtained the job as a secretary. But they have made no attempt to contact her as of yet."

"I see," replied Melvick. "Contact them and inquire if they intend to communicate with her. Ask them if they know she is to be married."

"Yes sir—Sir, I have the report on Reaol 10. It seems he was a bodyguard for Commander Aggo 1 but was detained for supposed activity of being involved with the opposition. He was sent to the reeducation center 1 year ago. He was released after 6 months and was then assigned to the *SS 927-C* to track down Commander Aggo 1 and capture him. He arrived at Starbase Outreach two days ago. It says here that that the captain and some of the crew were lost in a battle trying to capture Commander Aggo1. The ship returned with only a skeleton crew and Reaol 10 as acting first officer," Stener said as he put the report down.

"Very well, have Captain Mayer 3 and Lieutenant Hover 2 go to Repul and act as a newlywed couple. They must keep track of everything they do and try to find out what they are up to. Have them report back to me as soon as they find out anything."

"Yes sir," the director said as the phone clicked in his ear.

He then called Captain Mayer 3 and told him he was going on a mission with Lieutenant Hover 2. He explained the mission and said, "Remember you are there to follow Reaol 10 and his supposed new bride, not to . . . with Lieutenant Hover 2" He knew of Captain Mayer 3's reputation with women. "Keep track of everything they do and who they talk to. Find out what they are up to if possible. Become friends with them and stay with them everywhere they go. Stay with them at all times if you can. Never let them out of your sight. Report back to Melvick as soon as you find out anything." Stener placed the phone back in its cradle.

CHAPTER 14

When Hunter Reaol 10 and his new bride, Linda Chan-Reaol reached Repul, they went directly to the front desk to check in. After checking in they headed to the elevator, seeing another couple standing there discussing something. When they reached the elevator the other couple turned and looked at them, as if surprised to see them.

"Are you going to go to use this elevator?" Hunter asked them.

"Oh, yes. We were just discussing a few things," answered Lieutenant Hover 2 (Lacy) quickly, looking up at them as she said it. "I'm Lieu . . . " she stammered as Harvey Mayer 3 quickly bumped her arm.

"We were just discussing where we should go to eat tonight," her supposed husband said, glancing over at Lacy, his supposed new wife. "I'm Harvey Mayer 3 and this is my new bride Lacy Hover-Mayer. We were just married two days ago." He said by way of explanation, smiling as he said it.

"Yes that's me, Lacy Hover 3." She nervously tried to cover her slip. "I mean, I'm Lacy Hover-Mayer 2 . . . umm . . . 3 . . . Hover 2 . . . Mayer 3," she stammered. "And this is my new husband . . . ah . . . Harvey Mayer 3," she continued as she extending her hand.

"Glad to meet you," both Hunter and Linda said together as they shook their extended hands.

"I'm Linda Chan-Reaol and this is my husband Hunter Reaol 10. We were just on our way up to our room. Does this elevator work?"

"Oh! Yes," said Lacy, pressing the call button and smiling nervously at them. As they walked into the elevator she said, "We are on 3. What floor are you on?" She pushed the button for three.

"We are on also on 3," said Linda, as they stepped in the elevator with them.

When they reached their floor they discovered they were in rooms adjoining each other.

"Well . . . this is nice. See you later," said Lacy as they went into their room.

When Linda and Hunter had finished putting their clothes away, Linda took off her top and threw it on the bed. With a lilt in her voice, she grabbed Hunter's hand and said, "I'm going to have a bath. Join me."

"Um . . . sure, why not?"

Once in the bathroom, Linda said quietly after turning the shower on, "I don't trust them." She dropped her skirt and stepped into the shower. "Care to join me?" She motioned for Hunter to follow her. "Seeing as they said it would look better if I was pregnant when we went to MAMI headquarters," she said as she reached down and started stroking him, "we may as well start now."

"You sure changed a lot," he said caressing her.

"Well, we're married now, aren't we?" She gazed into his eyes. "I feel like I can do anything now. With you . . . " His lips closed over hers.

When they finished their shower and had dressed, they stepped into the hall just as Lacy and Harvey were coming out of their room—almost as if they had been listening for them.

"We are going down to get something to eat. Care to join us?" asked Harvey, looking at them as they stood smiling at each other.

When they reached the restaurant, they were quickly shown to a table. While they ate, Harvey started asking questions about where they worked, what they did, and how long they had known each other.

When Hunter replied his was in the Space Service, Harvey started asking questions about what he did. After finding out Hunter had just returned from a mission in space, he then started asking all kinds of questions about the mission.

"I'm sorry," said Hunter, giving him a sharp, penetrating look. "I can't talk about it."

"Oh . . . I see, secret stuff? Huh?" Harvey smiled at him. "OK. Is your job secret too?" he asked Linda, still smiling.

"Some of it," she said. "I'm just a temp secretary at the capital."

After they had finished their meal Harvey said, "Let's go dancing."

They all agreed and went to the club that was next door to the restaurant. They found a table and ordered drinks. Then leaving the drinks on the table, they all went out on the dance floor. After about an hour and after several drinks, Harvey asked Linda to dance, and Lacy asked Hunter to dance. After several dances with one another's partners, they all started walking back to their table.

Once they reached the table, Hunter asked Linda to dance. He put his arm around her shoulder and led her back onto the dance floor. They walked out to the dance floor with Harvey and Lacy right behind them. As they danced, they noticed that Harvey and Lacy were always next to or close by them at all times.

When the dance ended they again returned to their table. Hunter looked lovingly at Linda and said, "I think I will take my new wife for a little . . . stroll . . . in the moonlight."

"Fine," said Harvey, turning to them. "We'll join you. That is, if we may."

"Well . . . " Hunter said, looking at them. "That's not quite what I meant."

"Oh . . . I see." Harvey put his hand in his pocket and brought out a brooch that looked just like the one Lacy was wearing. "I got Lacy a brooch. When I gave it to her we discovered they had mistakenly put two in the sack instead of one. Would you please accept this other one?" he asked, offering it to Linda.

"But don't you want to return it?" asked Linda, trying not to be rude.

"I bought it in a little, inexpensive shop on the way here, and I don't really remember where it is." Harvey started to pin it to Linda's top—just above her left breast, close to her neck. His arm brushed her breast as he did.

"Well thank you," Linda said, looking at him and then at the brooch as he patted the top of her breast.

As soon as they had walked out of Harvey and Lacy's sight, Hunter reached over and unclasped the brooch from Linda's top and put it in his pocket.

Linda looked at him. "Why?" she started to ask.

"Later," Hunter replied giving her a stern look.

After walking and talking for most of an hour, they returned to their room. Hunter handed the brooch back to Linda. He explained to her earlier while they were walking that he thought the brooch was a bug,

Linda went into the bathroom, turned the water on in the sink, and dropped the brooch into the water. "Oops! It fell in the water as I was taking it off darling." She smiled at Hunter.

When they retrieved the brooch the following morning, Linda

asked, smiling at him, "Do you suppose it damaged it any? I'd rather they did not hear what we did last night."

When they walked out of their room, they were not surprised to find both Harvey and Lacy standing in the hall, closing their door as if they had just come out of their room. Dressed in beach attire, they had large smiles on their faces.

"Did you enjoy yourselves last night?" Harvey asked, still smiling at them.

"It looks like they may have," said Hunter quietly as he looked at Linda. "But not through that bug."

"We were just going to go eat. Would you care to join us?" asked Lacy, smiling at them. "You must have been tired last night." Lacy was saying as they walked down the hall. "We didn't hear a sound from your room. All night."

Linda and Hunter just smiled at each other.

"Maybe not," Linda said grinning up at Hunter.

While they were eating, Lacy asked. "What do you have planned for today?"

"Well . . . " said Linda a little shyly. "We thought we would go to the beach and . . . "

"And maybe have a picnic," said Harvey before Linda could continue. "I know a great place. We could get some food here from the restaurant and some blankets from the hotel and have a real picnic on the beach," he said happily.

"Well . . . I don't know," Linda said slowly as she looked at Hunter.

Hunter nodded slowly and said, "We would have to change into some different clothes first though. We're not dressed for the beach. We were just going sightseeing."

Linda just looked at him, her eyes roaming over him and said slowly to Harvey, smiling, "OK. How soon do you want to leave?"

"Good! I'll get the food from the kitchen and you go and change. Then we will be ready to leave. Fifteen minutes OK?" said Harvey, still smiling. He reached over and placed a hand on Linda's shoulder, caressing it softly. "We are all ready dressed for the beach, as you can see." He looked at Lacy sitting in her string bikini and cover-up that was giving a nice partial view of her large full breasts.

On their way to their room, Hunter laid his hand on Linda where Harvey had earlier and felt the bug on Linda's top. He then told Linda very quietly, keeping his hand on the bug, of his plan to get Harvey and Lacy to expose themselves if they were indeed there to spy on them.

"It should be fairly easy if you go along with me," he said as they stepped into their room. Taking Linda's clothing off and tossing it into a far corner, he said, "I wish you could go swimming like this."

"We'll see. Maybe we can. If you approve." Linda gave him a loving look as she changed into her swimsuit, which did not cover much.

"Anything you want," he said, understanding what she was saying.

After they had both changed, he asked if she had ever tried to influence other people's minds.

"No. I didn't know you could," she said, looking up at him.

"Well, not everyone can, and it is not general knowledge." He stepped into the bathroom and closed the door, turning the shower on and dropping the bug to the shower floor. "Stand here and I will show you how it is done." With that, Hunter stepped back from Linda and Harvey appeared, standing where Hunter had been.

Linda let out a small squeak and quickly covered her mouth.

Just as quickly as Harvey had appeared, Hunter reappeared and stepped close to Linda, putting his arms around her. "Sorry if I scared you. But now that you have seen how it is done, do you think you could do it?"

"You didn't scare me. You just startled me. I have been thinking of . . . with him and Lacy. I'll try. How do you do it?" she asked, still looking at him, startled. She regained her composure and stepped backwards.

"Well, you think really hard about what you want the other person to see or not see. And then try to place that thought in that person's mind. If it works, the other person will see what you want. Depending on how strong your mind is, you can influence people up 100 feet away. Further than that, for about another 150 feet, you just look fuzzy to the people who are looking at you. Beyond that, they see the real you.

"If you are really good at it, you can influence minds further away. Beyond a certain distance they will see the real you. So you have to be somewhat careful of where you are and what you are showing or not showing when you do it," Hunter continued saying as he looked into her eyes.

Linda stood with Hunter's hands on her shoulders and getting a very thoughtful look on her face. She changed into the image of Lacy, wearing the same clothes that they had seen her in that morning at breakfast—a string bikini and a transparent cover–up, complete with Lacy's large breasts but her smaller nipples. Just as quickly she disappeared and then reappeared with Lacy's face on her nude body, still with Hunter's hands on her shoulders. "Oops!" she squeaked, with a startled look on her face. She slowly disappeared and then reappeared again with her skirt on, looking like herself.

But lying on the floor was another small device, clearly having fallen from Linda's clothes. Looking at it, Hunter quickly recognized it as a transmitter. It had obviously been placed on Linda by either Lacy or Harvey when they had greeted them earlier.

"Sorry," she said turning red. "I meant to show you Lacy."

Hunter quickly put his hand over her mouth and pointed to the small transmitter, still lying on the floor of the shower. He bent down, picked it up, and took it over to the sink, saying as he went, "Sorry, it seems you can't influence other people's minds. I'm sorry that you made such a mess. You had better take a quick shower and wash your clothes off while you are at it."

He reached and turned the faucet on. After holding the transmitter under the faucet for a few minutes, he turned to Linda and said as he dried the transmitter off, "I should have told you. If you don't know what the other person's body looks like, your body will appear instead of theirs. So if you are thin and they are heavyset, you will appear as a thin them, or as a man instead of a woman." Hunter smiled at her and held her by the shoulders.

"But I do know what her body looks like. Did you not you look at her at breakfast?"

"Not really. I was busy looking at you," he answered. "So was Harvey."

She just smiled.

"I must say though, it was a surprise to see Lacy's face on your beautiful body," Hunter said smiling at her. "I like it better with your face on your body though."

She slapped him on the shoulder and said, "We'd better get ready and go."

"Yes, place this somewhere on your clothing. It is still working enough to show you still have it with you, but not well enough for them to hear all that is said." Hunter handed the transmitter back to her.

When they walked out of their room, they were surprised not to find Lacy or Harvey standing there waiting for them.

As they walked into the restaurant, they saw both Lacy and Harvey sitting at their table with a picnic basket and several bottles of wine. Hunter and Linda were both surprised, seeing Lacy had undone her sheer cover-up, allowing her large breasts to show through the opening, to be seen quite clearly. Since the cover-up had large arm holes, her breasts were completely visible when she leaned forward to stand when reaching for the picnic basket on the table.

"We're ready," said Lacy, pulling her cover-up closed again. She looked at Harvey with a bit of a smile as she did so.

"We are too," said Hunter as they started to leave the restaurant, looking at Linda's opaque cover-up.

"Where are we going?" asked Linda when they were out of the restaurant and walking toward the beach.

"Well, I thought we would go to this little cove Harvey and I found our first day here." Lacy said. Her cover-up had opened up again, showing most of her breasts as she turned toward them. They walked down the sidewalk to the beach talking, Lacy receiving many stares as they walked. "We will be able to sun and swim there and . . . with no one around to see us." Lacy smiled wickedly at Linda. "If you know what I mean." She pulled her top together again with one hand, but it fell completely open again as soon as she released it.

"Yes, I have heard how some couples . . . once they are married." Linda answered, smiling at Lacy.

The cove was a good forty-five to fifty minute walk from the resort. When they arrived, it proved to be well worth the effort it took to get there. They had had to walk mostly through the jungle trees and undergrowth on an almost invisible trail to reach it. The branches kept pulling Linda's cover-up completely open most of the way, allowing her breast to be exposed like Lacy's.

When they had reached the cliff, maybe twenty feet high overlooking the cove, they saw a small beach, about fifty feet wide with slightly higher cliffs on two sides that extended at least one hundred feet out into the sea. The cliffs dropped off sharply to the water, ending in a nice sandy beach. There was a wonderful view of the ocean as you looked out over it. As they made their way down a winding trail along the face of the cliff, Lacy and Linda both were saying to each other how lovely it was.

When they reached the beach, a small sailboat of about sixty feet rounded the far edge of the cliff and sailed toward the beach, coming in on its motors. When it dropped anchor about thirty feet out from the shore, two people, a young man and woman, stepped to the railing of the ship and dove over the side and swam to the beach. Laughing at each other, they splashed water on each other as they swam. They swam to shore, paying no attention to the couples on the beach.

As the man and woman walked out on to the beach, Linda and Hunter both quickly recognized Lisa—with a man neither of them knew.

"Hello," Lisa said, suddenly feigning surprise as they walked calmly came up the beach. She held out her hand to them as the water continued to drip off her full breasts, since all she was wearing was a small string-bottom that covered very little from the front and even less from the back.

"This is Alex Guard 2 and I am Lisa Guard 2. I hope we are not interrupting your day. We saw this cove yesterday as we sailed by and thought it would be a perfect place for a private day in the sun," she said as she looked up at her "husband" with adoring eyes. "We won't bother you . . . will we? We can always leave if you would rather we did." She looked at Hunter and Linda as if she did not know them. "You see, we were married one Cycle ago and thought we would have another honeymoon here. We loved it so much when we were here last Cycle."

"Well , ye . . . " Lacy started to object.

But Linda quickly interrupted saying, "No of course you're not. Please join us," she quickly replied with an invigorating smile. "Yes, please do join us," Lacy held her arms out, giving them a good look at her breasts as her cover-up came open. She leaned over to spread the beach blanket the resort had provided, allowing her cover-up to fall completely open, giving even a better view of her as she bent at the waist with her back toward them, her cover- up riding up well above her waist.

Hunter quickly set up the small canopy the resort had also provided.

"I'm Linda Chan 3, I mean Linda Chan-Reaol and this is Hunter Reaol 10, my new husband. We were just married 2 day ago," said Linda. "And that is Lacy and Harvey . . . I'm sorry, I don't remember your last names." She turned to look at Lacy and Harvey, her cover-up still hanging off her breasts completely open.

"I'm Lacy Hover 2 . . . Mayer, and this is my husband, Harvey

Mayer 3. I am Lacy Hover-Mayer, I should say." Lacy slowly took off what was left of her cover-up, letting it fall to the blanket since it had ripped considerably during their walk, showing all she had on was a small string-bottom also. "We have been married 4 days now, and I'm still not use to my new name." She quickly looked at Harvey with a smile and shrugged her shoulders, causing her full breasts to rise.

"We have plenty of food and wine." Lacy pointed to the basket Harvey was setting down on the blanket. "Won't you please join us?" she said as Harvey gave her a stern look that spoke volumes, mostly saying, *You shouldn't have invited them,* but also the look asked *how do we get rid of them now?* "Won't you please join us?" she said again as she turned back to Lisa.

"Well if you're sure?" Lisa walked up to us. Water still dripped off her firm breasts. "Alex, won't you please go back to the ship and get some more food and wine?" She finished saying this as she glanced at Linda, who had now taken off her cover-up, dropping it onto the blanket and was standing in her string-bottoms, which were as small as hers and Lacy's. She smiled and said, "Let's go and find some wood for a fire, Linda."

When they left, Lacy said quietly to Harvey, "What do we do now?" not realizing that Hunter could hear them. "We will never be able to seduce anything out of Hunter or Linda with *them* here." Lacy watched Linda and Lisa jogged to the tree line, their firm bodies jiggling as they ran. They reached the tree line and picked up dead wood for the fire.

"We can still try," Harvey said, watching Linda and Lisa as they ran.

Lacy started laying the food out on another blanket.

Harvey slid up next to Hunter and started asking questions—hinting that they should get rid of these new people, saying they would interfere with the plans he and Lacy had made for the day with them, giving Hunter a leering smile as he said it.

Hunter said he kind of enjoyed having them there. "You never know what may happen," he said with a equally leering smile.

Harvey started asking questions again about the Space Service, saying they had not had much chance to talk about it. He asked him about what he did there, this time asking where he went and what he saw and did while in space. "I think it would get boring," he said when Hunter started to look inquisitively at him.

"You can always find someone, I mean something to do," Hunter said, smiling at him. Hunter very carefully started telling him about how Space Service looked for different things that might be hazardous to travel and how they have helped people who were having trouble in space.

Harvey asked more and more questions, finally asking if he had been involved with the hunt for the reported traitor, Commander Aggo 1.

Hunter sat looking at Harvey with a stern expression on his face.

Harvey, trying to cover up any indication that he was unduly interested in the answer, quickly said, "I just thought that since you said you looked for people in space that maybe you had searched for him and could answer some of my questions about his guilt. I have my doubts about his guilt. I personally wonder if he is actually guilty or if he's being framed. I always thought he was a hero from his involvement in the last space conflict. And since you had said you had just returned from a mission, I thought maybe . . . "

"I cannot talk about that mission," Hunter said, still looking sternly at Harvey. "You do know all the news sources say he is guilty though. The last I heard they still have not caught him," Hunter said as Linda and Lisa walked back with their arms loaded with wood.

"We'll be right back." They dropped the wood in a pile and jogged back for more, hips swaying provocatively. When they reached the trees Linda quietly said to Lisa, "I've been bugged. Hunter tried to disable it but had to leave it working some so they did not get suspicious as to why it quit working too. They have tried several others. We can't be heard if we talk low and make a little background noise." She quickly went on to tell how they had found the bugs and what they done to disable them. But she did not tell Lisa what they had discovered she could do with her mind.

As they kept looking for wood, Lisa asked where the bug was.

Pointing to her feet she said, "It is on my shoe," then pointing to the pin on her string-bottoms, "and one on my . . ."

"OK. I have a plan. How do you fell about going nude?"

"Well, if I have to. Since the wedding I'm more . . . comfortable without clothing, and Hunter said I can . . . if I want to," Linda said. "I can't just take my shoes and bottoms off. They would get suspicious."

"I'll take care of that." Lisa leaned down and grabbed a large log said very loudly. "Help me."

As they were dragging the log back, Linda quietly asked Lisa why she and Alex were there and why they were using different names.

Lisa quickly explained, also very quietly, why she and Alex were there. They had found out that the MAMI were sending someone there to keep track of them and find out what they knew and maybe even take them into custody. Once Major Calm 27 had discovered this, he sent her and Captain Guardian to help them.

Lisa then explained how she and Alex were already as much of a couple as they could be since they had been together for over a Cycle. They were currently living together and were thinking of getting married later this Cycle.

"We thought it would be best not to use our real names." She finished saying.

Linda agreed.

As Lisa finished talking she "stumbled" and stepped on Linda's shoe, causing it to rip and come off.

"Oh, my shoe!" Linda exclaimed loudly.

"Sorry . . . It will be all right though." Lisa smiled at Linda. "I'll come back for it later. Just help me with this log," Lisa said as they continued dragging the log to the large pile of wood.

Linda quickly stepped out of her other shoe.

When they dropped the log, Lisa let it slide down her thigh, catching her string tie and pulling it loose, causing her bikini to start coming off as she turned. Apparently not noticing, she ran for Linda's shoes, picked them up, and came running back. "I'm sorry. It looks like I ruined your shoes." She handed them to Linda.

As she took the shoes from Lisa, Linda looked down at Lisa's string that had slipped halfway down her leg, exposing her hairless body. "I think you're losing something," she said to Lisa.

"Oh . . . oh, yes . . . right," Lisa said lightly as she looked down at her bottoms and reached for the tie, pulled it loose, then tossed the string onto a blanket, as Alex came running up the beach carrying their food and drink.

"We were going to tan in the nude on the beach anyway, and now that you have seen all of me, I might as well stay nice and tan. Won't you all join me?" She looked around at everyone as Alex sat the food down and then dropped his swim suit, smiling at Lisa.

"Oh well," said Linda. She took her "ruined" shoes and tossed them into the fire, which was just starting to burn well. "I guess if you are going to tan, we may as all get tan too, right Hunter?" She untied her string-bottom and pulled it off, throwing it down next to Lisa's. Completely uncaring.

"No don't!" yelled Lacy as the shoes started to burn. "I could have fixed them for you." She watched them burn.

"Oh well, they are just cheap shoes," Linda said, shrugging her shoulders. "I can get another pair back at the resort." She turned to Lacy. "Won't you join us?" Lacy tried reaching for the shoes. "You'll burn yourself," she said as Lacy leaned close to the fire, almost burning her breasts and fingers.

"Well," she said, looking at Harvey who was brushing at her breasts, which had gotten hot as she leaned in to retrieve the shoes. Harvey then started stepping out of his suit. "I guess if everyone else is . . ." she said as she took off her string and threw it with both other girls'.

As the day went on on both Harvey and Lacy continued to take every opportunity they could to question both Hunter and Linda about their flight and their hurried marriage, being very suggestive with their bodies as the talked.

"If you ever want to talk about anything, please contact me at the capital. I'll give you my number when we get back to the resort," Harvey said after talking to Hunter for at least an hour. "I will see that you get to speak to the right people. I'm sure they will be a great help to you."

As the sun was setting, Lisa said to them all after they had been talking and tanning all afternoon, "Won't you all join us on our boat for the trip back to the resort?"

CHAPTER 15

Four weeks later, Captain Mayer 3 and Lieutenant Hover 2 were standing in front of Director Stener, giving him a full report as to what had went on during the honeymoon. They told him how they had met Linda and Hunter at the resort and how they had planted several bugs on Linda, but they had all seemed to quit working after about an hour after they left them.

They then went on to tell how they had invited Linda and Hunter down to a secluded beach—their plan being to seduce them and get information. That, they explained, had not quite worked the way they had planned. They explained that they had been interrupted by a couple named Lisa and Alex Guard, and that Linda and Hunter had made fast friends with them. After that, neither he nor Lacy had been able to get either of them completely alone and were unable to *talk* to either Linda or Hunter in private.

They also told him that whenever they saw either Hunter or Linda, Lisa or Alex were always with them. They would hear them in the room all night *talking*. It seemed like they had moved in with them. They were with them all the time. They even told Director Stener how they had tried to seduce them when they would meet them in the morning for a meal. Lisa and Alex would be there and they would go back to the room with them when they went to get ready for the day's activities. They even went back to the room at night with them.

They had managed to get Hunter and Linda to go back to the secluded beach several times, but they would always have to take Lisa and Alex's boat, saying it was quicker. They would then get nude as soon as they left the dock, thus not giving Harvey or Lacy a chance to plant any more bugs on them.

When Captain Mayer 3 had completed his report, Stener turned to Lieutenant Hover 2 and asked her for her report. Lieutenant Hover 2 gave her report, which varied only slightly from Captain Mayer 3's.

Stener sat back in his chair behind his big desk and looked thoughtfully at them standing in their uniforms. He then said with a stern look on his face, "You should have been able to find some way to get them alone.

"Couldn't you get Hunter alone?" He looked at the lieutenant, sitting in her uniform, which stopped just above her full large breasts. "Stand up," he said suddenly. "Take your uniform off," he added as she stood.

Lieutenant Hover 2 looked at Captain Mayer 3, then stood up and proceeded to remove her uniform while giving Harvey sideways glances as she did. She removed the last piece of clothing and turned around after placing it on the chair behind her, unaware of the leering, looks Stener had been giving her as she did so. Turning slowly back around, she stood with just her shoes on, now aware of the leering looks from Stener. But she stood silently, standing at attention and staring straight ahead out the window as people walked by. Occasionally, a passerby would stop and look in at her as she stood.

"Yes . . . yes." he said finally, as he looked at Lieutenant Hover 2, still standing at attention. "Yes." He was still giving her leering looks. "I see no reason why you should not have been able to seduce the information for him."

She turned her head slightly to look at Harvey who, was looking at her too. He just shrugged his shoulders slightly.

"Very well." Stener waved his hand at her and finally looked down at some papers on his desk. "You may put your uniform back on." He waved at her to put her clothes on—but had a slightly ashamed look on his face. "Hmm," he said, looking back up at Lieutenant Hover 2 as she was getting dressed and then fluffing her hair. "We will have to do something about those uniforms. They show entirely too much." His face went slightly red.

"But . . ." Lieutenant Hover 2 started to say, but quickly stopped when she saw the look on Stener's face. Just then, there was a sudden knock on his door. "Quick," he said. They did not need to know who it was. He pointed to a door on the far side of the room. "Go! You must not be seen here."

After they had both left through the door, Stener placed the papers out of sight in his desk. He calmly went to the outer office door, since he had dismissed his secretary earlier, and opened it to find both Linda and Hunter.

"Won't you come in? How may I help you?" he asked politely as he stood there in the doorway looking at Linda in her semi-transparent top.

CHAPTER 16

Lisa and Alex walked into Major Calm 27's office still dressed in the clothing they had been wearing while on Repul with Hunter and Linda.

"How did it go?" asked the major, looking from the papers on his desk to Lisa in her sheer top and very short skirt.

"Fine," replied Captain Guardian. "Everything is going according to plan. They should be arriving at the MAMI offices about now." He glanced at the clock on the wall.

"Good, good. You made sure both Hunter and Linda know the plan?" he asked.

"Yes sir," said Lisa with a grin. "We went over it several times with both Linda and Hunter before we left.

"You're sure Captain Meyer 3 and Lieutenant Hover 2 do not suspect anything?"

"Very sure," replied Lisa with a smile on her face and looking at Alex. "We took every precaution we could to make sure we were not overheard. Besides, they thought we were doing something besides talking," she said, smiling at Alex.

"I don't want to know," said the major, looking at them smiling at each other. "Then we will proceed with the next step of the plan." He reached for the phone on his desk. As he dialed, he looked at Lisa and Alex smiling at each other with their completely suntanned bodies and said, "It seems like you both enjoyed this assignment."

He suddenly said into the phone, "Tell Victor the word is go."

He looked again at Lisa and Alex. "I'm surprised you had time to do any thinking or anything else judging from your tans," he continued on saying as if it had all been one conversation.

"Well," Alex said sheepishly, we had to spend a lot of time outside to keep Captain Meyer 3 and Lieutenant Hover 2 from hearing everything had to tell Hunter and Linda. It took a lot of time and creative thinking to get them alone long enough to explain everything.

"It took a lot of *creative* thinking to get them alone long enough to explain things." Lisa said, giving the major a sly look.

"I'll bet it did," said the major. Looking to Lisa he said, "You shouldn't have spent so much time on your back, Lisa. Your back is a little lighter than your front."

At this he reached under his desk and turned the White Noise Device off that had been playing the sounds of him still busy rustling papers on his desk.

There was a knock on his door.

"Just a minute." He held up his hand to Alex and Lisa motioning for them to be seated.

"Thank you for stopping in, Lieutenant Distain 8 and you too, Captain Guardian. I'm glad you are back from your leave. I'll see you tomorrow morning, Lieutenant. Don't forget we will be in our temporary offices while they renovate these old ones."

"Yes sir." She got up, walked to the office door, and opened it.

"The major will see you now," she said as she held the door open for Abbrelle, Christy and me.

"Lieutenant!" said the major as he motioned them all to come in and be seated. "You are still on leave until tomorrow."

"Yes sir, sorry sir. Habit. I'll be in at 07:00 tomorrow," she said as she closed the door and returned to her seat.

"Be seated, all of you, I'll be with you in a few minutes." He reached under the desk again and turned the switch to the White Noise Device back on again.

"Linda and Hunter should be at MAMI headquarters now," he said to us after a few seconds.

While I took notice of Lisa's tan, the girls looked at Alex's sunburned back, smiling. It didn't take much to figure out what they had been doing, but with whom was the question.

"I believe it is now time to place into operation the plans we have been discussing. Your transportation to the capital has all been arranged. Our people at the capital are waiting for you to arrive to set the plan into motion." He then stood up and held his hand out to Abbrelle, Christy, and me. "Good luck," he said as he shook each of our hands. He reached under the desk an turned the Device off.

"Now," he said. "Lieutenant Distain 8 has brought word of a sighting of Aggo 1. He was sighted off the coast on a small island near the Island of Repul. You are to go there and check it out at once. If it is true, do not attempt to capture him unless it can be done with little risk to yourselves and with little chance of failure. Here is the report," he said as the handed the paperwork that he had been working on to Abbrelle.

Abbrelle looked at the blank papers with a questioning look and handed them to Christy and I. When the major reached back under the desk and turned the Device back on, it dawned on me what he was doing and that he had more to say.

The major held his hand out for the blank papers and said, "Proceed to the capital immediately and implement plan Omega. May all of the gods be with you," he said, looking at us.

"Now let us proceed over to the temporary offices so they can move everything out of here." He said getting up. "I'll see you in the morning Lieutenant."

When we were outside, he told us everything Lisa and Alex had discovered about Captain Harvey Meyer 3 and Lieutenant Lacy Hover 2 while they were with Linda and Hunter and how they had had to run interference so they did not have to spend all their time answering questions about themselves. He also told how they had used the sounds of them talking to cover the sounds of them talking.

CHAPTER 17

As we sat in the boarding lounge, waiting for the plane to the Capital to take off, a middle-aged lady stood hesitantly next to Christy, looking at the only vacant chair left next to her. She asked Christy is it was saved for anyone.

"Yes . . . of course. I was saving it just for you," said Christy as she removed her belongings from the seat and smiled at the woman. "Please, sit down." She stared intently into the woman's face. "Do I know you?" she asked, still looking at her.

"No, I don't think so," was the reply.

"But you look like someone I know," she said, still staring at her as she sat down.

"I use to hear that a lot before my daughter left," she said sadly, looking back at Christy.

"Then you must be Linda Chan 3's mother," said Christy excitedly.

Suddenly staring at Christy, "Yes . . . how did you know her name was Linda though? She never uses it." She looked at Christy who turned and looked at us questioningly, not knowing what to say.

Both Abbrelle and I just shrugged our shoulders, wondering how they had come up with Linda's correct name.

"Well . . . " stammered Christy. "You know she is married now, don't you?"

"Yes . . ." Mrs. Chan 2 replied, wondering how this stranger would know that. "I'm on my way to meet with her boss and see if she will talk to me."

"Well, I'm Christy Emulate 3, and this is my sister Abbrelle Emulate 2,and our friend Steve.

"And Hunter is . . . " she starting to say when Abbrelle jabbed her in the ribs, shaking her head *no*. " . . .our best friend," Christy quickly said, trying to cover her slip.

"Yes, we have known him for years," Abbrelle quickly said, trying to fill in the error as she looked at Christy with a dark look on her face.

"Too much information," Abbrelle mouthed silently to Christy.

"Oh . . . oh . . . my goodness. Really?" Mrs. Chan 2 gasped. "Really?" she said over and over. "I'm her mother, I'm very glad to meet you. I had no idea I would meet some of Reaol 10's friends since I don't even know him," she said as she turned to look at Christy again with a big smile starting on her face. "Please, what can you tell me about him? Did they have a nice wedding? Are they happy? How long has she known him? . . . are they happy? . . . Are they?"

"Slow down. We will answer what questions we can since we did not make it to the wedding." Christy smiled at her and then at Abbrelle who was also getting excited. With that, a discussion started that lasted all the way to the capital. She and Christy sat next to each other on the plane, and Abbrelle and I were seated across the aisle from them, also answering questions as they talked. No one seemed to remember Christy's near slip earlier of almost letting her know that they were Hunter's sisters.

When we landed at the capital, Christy asked if someone was meeting her or if she needed a ride. "We would be happy to take you wherever you need to go."

"Someone is to meet me."

They walked into the terminal and saw a woman in a military uniform holding a sign that said "Mrs. Chan 2." "Oh that must be for me," she said, walking over to the women with the sign. As they stood talking they both turned and looked at us. The woman with the sign stared at Abbrelle as if concentrating as to where she knew her. Her mouth fell agape as she recognized her.

Abbrelle looked back at her, and turned slightly to Christy. "I should know her. I know I have seen her before, But where . . . ."

"Yes, so should I," answered Christy. They continued staring at the woman. A look of sudden recognition came to Christy's face as it lit up with a smile.

The driver still had a strange look on her face while slowly walking toward Abbrelle, with Mrs. Chan 2 walking beside her with a look of wonderment on her face.

"That's Hover 2. Remember Abbrelle, from school? She was in your grade," said Christy to Abbrelle.

"Oh . . . yes!" Abbrelle smiled with sudden recognition . She took off at a fast walk and met Lieutenant Hover 2 halfway, threw her arms around her and said, "Hover 2, it has been so long. It's good to see you again. You left right after school. Look at you know, a lieutenant and working at the capital of all places. It's good to see you. How have you been?"

"Emulate 2? Is it really you?" Lieutenant Hover 2 was astonished but overjoyed to see her as she hugged her back, truly happy to see her. "The last I heard . . . we can't talk here," she whispered quietly in her ear as she continued to hug her. "Come with me."

Motioning for us to follow, she headed to the family restroom holding a finger to her lips for silence. Reaching the restroom, she opened the door and waved us all in. She closed the door and held a finger to her lips again when Abbrelle started to speak. She reached into her purse and removed a small device, which we instantly recognized as a White Noise Device, only a smaller version. It was similar to the one Lisa had used back in the offices when we first landed. Nodding her head, Abbrelle instantly closed her mouth and motioned for us all to be quiet.

When the device was activated, Lieutenant Hover 2 looked happily at Abbrelle and asked, "Emulate 2, do you still work for Commander Aggo 1 like I have heard?" she asked nervously.

"Why?" asked Abbrelle, suddenly looking at her with interest. "Where did you hear that?"

"Please just answer me. *Please*, " she said as she quickly looked at the device resting on the counter. "We only have about 20 minutes. I read that you and your sister here and your brother . . . "—suddenly realizing who her brother was. "Oh. Reaol 10." She looked at Mrs. Chan 2 and then clasped her hand over her mouth in surprise.

"She does not know does she . . . that he is your brother?" she asked, still looking at Abbrelle as Mrs. Chan 2 got a startled look on her face.

"Not yet, she didn't, but she does now," answered Christy, looking quickly from Lieutenant Hover 2 to Mrs. Chan 2.

"Well, she does now!" Abbrelle answered. Mrs. Chan 2 stared at them as the knowledge slowly dawned on her face.

"Why shouldn't I know who Reaol 10 is? Is he wanted or . . . ? Oh, he is your brother isn't he?" she asked as realization suddenly dawned on her face. "That is why you tried to cover your slip up, earlier, is it not. You didn't want me to know. What are you trying to hide?"

"Well, " said Christy, not looking directly at her.

"Are you here to rescue them? If so, I can help. I'm going to take a chance and trust you." Lieutenant Hover 2 looked at both of them with a questioning look on her face as it suddenly hit her. "You are, aren't you? Well we had better hurry. They are planning on using her," she said, pointing to Mrs. Chan 2, "to get some answers from them. I overheard them talking about it as I was leaving. I've had doubts about Director Stener and I have made up my mind to help you if you are trying to help . . . Hunter and Linda. If I'm wrong it means prison or worse for me."

"Why should we believe you?" asked Abbrelle. "The Hover 2 I knew in school was all about herself. Why should we believe you have changed now?"

"I know it will be hard for you to believe me," said Lacy, looking sadly at the floor. Then suddenly a small smile appeared on her face. "Do you remember when we were in grade school and we would say Cinderella swear?—meaning we could not break it or tell."

"Yes?" Abbrelle answered, looking at Lacy.

"Well, I Cinderella swear that I have decided to do everything I can to get rid of Director Stener and his party and to help you."

"What has my daughter done? What has she got herself into?" Mrs. Chan 2 looked at them suspiciously. "Is she OK?"

"She's fine. It's just . . . " answered Lacy."

"What?" Linda's mother asked anxiously.

"It's just about Reaol 10 . . . they think he is a spy," Lacy replied hastily.

"What makes them think so, Hover 2?" asked Christy.

"Call me Lacy," she said.

"I'm Christy, she's Abbrelle, and this is Steve," said Christy as she pointed at us.

"Where are Hunter and Linda?" Abbrelle asked, stepping forward.

"They're safe, for now. They are at the State House talking to Director Stener." Lacy answered. "I'm to bring Mrs. Chan 2 there."

Abbrelle looked at Lacy thoughtfully. "OK, we'll trust you, for now. How do we save them?"

"Well, it will not be easy." Lacy said. "But I think we can . . ."

They spent the next fifteen minutes discussing how they would save them, with Abbrelle and Christy trying to work their plan into the discussion without letting Lacy know that what they wanted was for

Hunter and Linda to get deeper into the headquarter building so they could get at the proof they needed to bring the whole group down.

When the timer on the face of the device showed we only had one minute left, Lacy asked, "Do you know the park near the capitol building? "We can meet there at 18:30 hours tonight."

"OK. We will meet you, but remember this all under Cinderella swear," Abbrelle said.

"Cinderella swear," repeated Lacy, nodding her head.

"What is . . ." Christy started to ask but Abbrelle held up a hand and said, "Later," causing Christy to close her mouth part way through the question.

We shut off the device with just ten seconds left on the timer, and left the restroom.

In the hallway, Christy, holding Mrs. Chan 2's arm, suddenly asked, "Are you alright now?"—as a woman and her three children came up to the family restroom.

"Yes," she said, trying to look as if she had been ill. "It must have been something I ate before I left. I'm alright now. Thank you." She said looking at Christy and patting her hand.

"Glad we could help," I said as we started to walk away. The woman gave me a strange look as she and her children walked by and into the restroom.

As Lieutenant Hover 2 headed for the car to take Mrs. Chan 2 to meet Hunter and Linda, Christy and Abbrelle both stood watching them leave, commenting on how nice Linda's mother was.

"I hope we get to meet her again under different circumstances," said Christy.

"I'm sure we will," said Abbrelle "But for now we can't let anyone know who we are."

The girls quickly altered their looks.

As we walked out of the terminal and saw them getting in a government car, Mrs. Chan 2 gave us a quick smile before they drove away.

"Come on," said Abbrelle. "We have things to do." She waved down a ground car.

CHAPTER 18

When we had checked into our hotel next to the park, I started putting our things away.

Christy knocked on the door connecting the two rooms and walked in, not waiting for me to answer, followed closely by Abbrelle.

"What would you have done if I hadn't been dressed?" I asked.

"Well, you are dressed, aren't you? It is not like we . . . " said Christy.

"We would have thought of something." Abbrelle smiled at me devilishly.

"Where are we going to hide these weapons?" They held the weapons they had been carrying.

"Well, for now," I said, opening a dresser drawer that had a lock on it, "I think here will do. When we leave, you two will have to have large purses to carry them in."

"I saw a shop in the lobby. I'll go down now and get a couple." Christy walked back into their room, then out again.

Abbrelle and I walked to the large sliding glass door and out on to the patio. I said, "We should be able to see all of the park from here."

"Yes, this will be a good place to watch from and work on my tan." She smiled slightly. "As we watch, of course."

"Your deck would be fine," I said, looking mischievously at her.

"I thought here would be better." She said with a downcast look on her face.

"Yes, here would be fine, wouldn't it?" I put my arms around her and drew her close to me.

She was smiling brightly as she put her arms around my neck, turning to hold me tightly—kissing me.

We stood on the deck like that admiring . . . the view . . . until Christy walked back into the room holding two large purses and a briefcase.

"I saw this and thought it would help with your disguise as a businessman." She held up the briefcase. Then she stopped suddenly as she looked at us. We had become very quite as we stepped apart and turned around.

"Did I interrupt something," she said smiling at her sister.

"No . . . no. Not yet," stammered Abbrelle, turning red.

"No . . . not a thing." I looked at Christy with a frown.

"We should be able to get the bigger weapons in here." Christ pointed at the briefcase.

"Yes," I said. "And as they are all plastic they shouldn't set off any alarms."

"What is . . . *plastic* . . . ?" Abbrelle asked.

"I know," Christy said, as I opened my mouth, smiling, "you'll explain later, right?"

"You got it." I said, laughing as I smiled at her.

"Your . . . language is strange." Abbrelle turned and looked out at the sliding glass door again, suddenly going rigid.

"Look," she said, pointing toward the park.

A small group of people had just walked out of the capital. Three of who were Hunter, Linda, and her mother, Martha. Martha glanced our way, and seeing Abbrelle, she gave a slight nod of her head indicating we should come over. We hurriedly left our room and quickly made our way to the park, entering the park before the group had walked one hundred feet into it. We met them near the middle of the park, all of us pretending to taking in the beauty of it.

"Well hello, Steve. Nice to see you again." Martha said, then she looked at Abbrelle and Christy, hiding her surprise at not recognizing them through their "glimmer" disguises, but knowing their voices as they both said "hello."

"Well hello, Mrs. Chan 2, fancy meeting you here," I said, holding my hands out to her and acting surprised to see her. "I didn't expect to see you here."

As she held my hands, she smiled at Linda and quietly said, "This is my daughter Linda Chan 3 and her new husband, Hunter Reaol 10." She turned slightly. "And this is Director Stener and Lieutenant Hover 3. These other gentlemen, I don't know." She said, sternly indicating the remaining four gentlemen standing around them, watching us closely.

"I met Steve here on the plane. He helped me when I got sick," she said to Director Stener, but mainly for Hunter and Linda's benefit— to show that we knew Mrs. Chan 2.

"Pleased to meet you sir and you ladies," the director said, bowing slightly to us.

"I was glad I could help her," I replied and started to hold out my hand, but instead gave him the same slight bow when he showed no sign of accepting my hand.

"And these ladies are Abbrelle and Christy," indicating them standing beside me. I had no fear their names would be recognized.

"No formal names?" He asked, looking at me questioningly.

"No." I gave him a sharp look. "They don't feel they are need."

"Ah, Ah, . . . of course," he answered again with a slight bow. "Business associates."

"You, could say that." I gave him a pleased look.

"Are you staying here long?" asked Martha.

"That depends on how long my business takes." I replied, still holding her hand and smiling, "and . . ." I said, looking at both Abbrelle and Christy.

"Maybe the director could help you," she said.

"Yes," the director said, looking at Abbrelle and Christy. "Come see me if there is anything I can help you with or tell my secretary where you are staying." He smiled at me. "And I will get in touch with you."— Although I knew he had seen us come from the resort.

"Excuse us, but we must be going." He placed a hand firmly on Martha's back and tried to steer her away.

"Don't . . ." she started to say, suddenly pulling away, but stopped when she saw the look and the slight shake of her head that Linda was giving her.

"It's all right Mother." Linda stepped up to her and put her arms around her. "He was not going to hurt you." She lifted Director Stener's hand off her back. "Since she was young, she hates to be touched." She gave him a pleading look as way of explanation.

"Yes, of course. I'm sorry," the Director said with a slight smile and a nod, dropping his hand down. "Shall we?" he said holding his arm out indicating the way to go. "Shall we go?" he said again firmly.

Giving him a slight nod of her head, Martha proceeded to walk away beside him saying as she went. "I hope we meet again Steve, Abbrelle, Christy," nodding to each of us as they left. Four men followed after them closely. One placed his hand to his lapel before he left and turned toward us for a second, leaving his hand on his lapel. I somehow knew he was taking our picture, so I smiled at him as he did.

When we were back in the rooms I said, "We'll have to be

careful what we say from now on in here," indicating the rooms. "They will probably have bugged the rooms by now. I was one of them talking to a hidden microphone. I know I would. And that last agent took our pictures.

"I know," said Abbrelle, shivering. "That means they would have known who Christy and I were if you hadn't suggested that we alter our appearance," she said as both she and Christy allowed their normal faces to reappeared, with a slight blurring as they did so.

"You know we were photographed quite frequently while with Commander Aggo 1."

We walked to the dresser drawer, pulled a small electrical device out, and started sweeping the rooms, looking for hidden bugs.

"Can't be to safe." I returned the device to the drawer. "I will have to find a better hiding place for all of these." I said, referring to the weapons and devices in the drawer.

"Shall we go find something to eat?" I asked Abbrelle and Christy once I had finished sweeping the room.

CHAPTER 19

When we returned it was obvious that the rooms had been searched and bugged. I quickly ran the scanner and found listening devices with cameras in every room including the bathrooms, allowing them to see . . . everything. I quickly deactivated them. But not before telling the girls to hold their "glimmer."

Once I had deactivated all of them, I said to the girls. "We can't let them get a true look at either of you. You can drop your 'glimmer' now."

We then spent several hours going over our plans and deciding what changes we would have to make to them.

Christy stood up and stretched her arms above and behind her head, thrusting her firm, uncovered breasts out. "I'm going to bed."

"I think I will too." Abbrelle said as she lay back on my bed. "See you in the morning," she said as Christy walked out, smiling the whole time at Abbrelle and I.

We were awakened at 05:30 the next morning by a quiet tap on the door. We both came instantly awake. Grabbing a towel from the bathroom, I barely got it around myself before peering out to see who was there. Seeing it was Lieutenant Hover 2, I opened the door wider and let her quickly slip in as I held the towel tight and looked up and down the hall to see if anyone was there.

"Oh," gasped Lacy upon seeing Abbrelle sitting up in my bed with the sheet down around her hips, her naked breasts out. "Sorry, did I interrupt something?" She turned slightly red.

"No." I grabbed our shorts from the floor and threw Abbrelle's to her. I put mine on while still looking at Lacy.

"That's something I have not seen before," she said, smiling at me as my towel fell. I pulled the shorts up and looked back at Abbrelle as she swung her legs over the edge, got out of my bed, and started putting her shorts on.

"I just found out that Director Stener is taking all of them to MAMI headquarters this morning. Here are tracking devices for the transmitters that I gave to Hunter, Linda, and Martha." She handed one to each of us, as Christy had came in from the other room with a towel held loosely in front of her otherwise nude body. "I have to hurry. I am to go to the office and meet them now. The transmitters are disguised as jewelry." She turned and started for the door.

"How soon?" I asked.

"About 15 minutes," she replied looking at her watch.

"I've got to go. They know you deactivated the bugs," she added as she hurried out the door. "They are trying to figure out who you are. They don't believe you are just a businessman."

We quickly dressed and went to the vehicle we had rented the night before. We were sitting outside the resort when a vehicle turned from the capital complex on to the street in front of us and sped off toward the MAMI Headquarters, apparently not looking to see whether they were being followed or not. We learned later, to our dismay, that if we had paid closer attention, we would have noticed that as we followed the car, another car pulled out and followed us.

We arrived at headquarters, which was ten miles outside of the city. We pulled over under some trees and got out of the car and started to walk toward the building, hidden among the trees. Walking around trees that surrounded the complex, trying to approach undetected, we failed to notice the car that had parked one hundred yards behind us.

Standing by the trees, just out of sight, we saw the car pull into the headquarters building driveway and Hunter being helped from the car. He seemed groggy, apparently drugged. He was closely followed by both Linda and Martha, who also acted as if they had been drugged. After watching them being taken quite forcibly into the complex, we quickly followed, staying just out of sight but not losing them.

When we reached the doors with our weapons drawn, I commentated on there not being a sentry posted.

"I saw him help carry Hunter in," said Christy.

"I don't like it." We walked in, trying to be inconspicuous.

We hid behind a corner and watched them being taken into a room halfway down the hallway.

I suddenly felt something pressed into the back of my neck. Reaching behind me, I felt a weapon. I calmly tapped Abbrelle on the shoulder. When she waved me off I said, "I think we have company." Since I wasn't trying to be quiet, both Abbrelle and Christy turned sharply around and stared at me as I stood there with my hands up.

"We suspected you would follow," said Lieutenant Blather 3 as he stood with the with weapon pointed at us.

"Good, you have them. Bring them here," said Captain Mayer 3 as he walked back down the hallway to us from the room where they had taken Hunter, Linda and Martha.

We were led into the room and saw them all sitting on chairs— Hunter, Linda, and Martha. Lacy was busy tying their hands behind their backs.

Harvey watched how sloppily Lacy was tying their hands. He gave her a stern look and said, "I thought you had gotten quite friendly with her," pointing at Abbrelle, "but I had hoped I was wrong." Looking hurt, he motioned for Lacy to join us against the wall. "You are tying them awfully loose. And it took a long time for you to come in this morning,"

"No . . . what? No, you don't understand," Lacy pleaded with him, seeing the suspicion in his eyes as he stared at her. "I stopped and told them so they would follow us. So we could catch them, just like you had planned," she said, shaking her head as she tried to convince him.

"Nice try, and I was getting to . . . like . . . you too." He backhanded her, knocking her to the floor. Walking over to where he had hit her, he reached down and lifted her chin. A bruise was quickly starting to develop on her cheek where he had struck her. Raising her face he looked down at her and scowled. "I don't believe you," he said as he reached for the collar of her uniform top, ripping it open, and pulling a small bug from under the lapel where it had been attached. "It will be a shame to send you to the reconditioning center. You won't be the same when you get out. You won't remember any of this." He dropped his hand onto her large, firm breast and pinched her nipple before releasing it, leering at her as he did it. "I did enjoy our little . . . trip though."

She turned her head, pulling away from him as he did, not looking at him so he could not see the hatred in her eyes.

"Why are you here? What were you planning to do?" He grabbed Hunter roughly by the hair and pulled his head so far back that we could see the blank look still in his dull eyes. He released his grip on Hunter's hair and let his head fall back down limply to his chest, seeing that he was still under the influence of the drug he had received during the trip.

Stepping over to Linda, he reached for her hair to pull her head back too when she suddenly lifted her head. Her eyes, raised, looked directly into his. Then she totally disappeared, leaving him standing there looking astonished as her ropes fell to the floor.

Gasping, he lunged against the chair with his arms out, trying to find her.

Feeling movement against my arm, I turned and saw his weapon floating next to me. At the same time Lieutenant Blather 3 suddenly slumped to the floor unconscious. Grabbing the weapon, I spun back around to hold it on Captain Mayer 3 just as he noticed Lieutenant Blather 3 hit the floor.

I saw Hunter stand up quickly behind Harvey and apply a nerve pinch, causing him to slump to the floor. Hunter took his weapon as he fell and held it as he stood looking at us.

"I thought it was you when they said we were being followed," he said. "They drugged us shortly after we got in the car." He looked over at Martha. When he stepped closer to her he bumped into Linda as she popped back into sight, standing next to her mother. "When did you learn to do that?" he asked Linda.

"Well, when we were practicing, I saw how you shimmered and changed. But I disappeared when I did it. Sooo . . . I just tried to do it slower and practiced whenever I was alone."

She looked worriedly down at her mother.

Her mother smiled at her and said, "I wondered how long it would take for you to figure out what you can do." Then looking at us, she said, "She scared the daylights out of me the first time she pulled that trick when she was little. I also see you were not affected by the drugs either," she said, disappearing and reappearing standing next to Linda.

"What—How—Mother!" Linda exclaimed as her mother stood there looking at her.

"I found out when I had you that drugs had no effect on me," her mother said, smiling as Linda stood there open-mouthed. "I have always been able to phase in and out.

"You never . . . " Linda started to say.

"Is that what it is called?" I asked, looking at her.

"Yes," she answered. Holding up her hand Martha said, "Now is not the time. I presume you have things to do." Just then, a group of armed men rushed into the room, all holding weapons and training them on us. As we stood there looking at them, Mrs. Wilde 4 stepped into the room followed closely by Chancellor Aggo 2.

Seeing Miss Chan 3, he quickly walked to her and said, "How are you, Miss Chan 3, I didn't mean for you to get caught up in this. Please forgive me. Did they do anything to you?"

"Thank you, sir. I would like you to meet my husband, Hunter Reaol 10, and my mother, Martha Chan 2." She held Hunter's arm tightly to her chest and looked up at him.

"Ah, yes. That was quite some scheme Major Calm 27 came up with." He nodded to Hunter.

"It was no scheme, Chancellor. She is my wife," Hunter said sternly. Then shifting his eyes down to Linda and slowly smiling at her, he said, "The papers have been filled."

"Have they? Are you sure? Well . . . be that as it may." As he was talking twenty more men led by Commander Aggo 1 started filling the small room.

"Hello Dad, nice you could make it." Chancellor Aggo 2 said as he turned to him and saw his father's men all had their weapons drawn and aimed directly at him. "I hoped this would get you out of hiding. You can drop your guns now."

"Why should we?" The commander asked as Linda and her mother both disappeared quietly.

"Because if you don't, this room will be filled with gas," the chancellor said, looking very unhappy.

"You will be gassed too," I said to him. He looked nervous now, looking around as if he hadn't thought of that.

"Well, what about the women? You don't want them to be gassed, do you?" the chancellor asked, trying to find a way out.

I just shrugged my shoulders. "What about them?"

"What! Where are Miss Chan 3 and her mother?" The chancellor looked around suddenly. As his weapon was wrenched from his hand and pointed at his head, Mrs. Wilde 4 hit the floor unconscious.

CHAPTER 20

"Stand still, all of you." It was Linda's voice, seemingly coming from above and behind a weapon that floated in the air.

Commander Aggo 1 grabbed the weapon from the air where it appeared to be floating. As he did, Melvick, closely followed by Director Stener, stepped into the room with weapons out and pointed at us.

"I believe you are the ones who should drop your weapons," Melvick said as he and Director Stener blocked the doorway.

"I think you have that wrong," I pointed my weapon at them.

Melvick looked at me and started to say, "If you don . . ." I shot him in the arm.

"Biggest mistake people make is that they talk too much. Drop your weapons," I said to Director Stener as Melvick had dropped his weapon, clasping his injured arm.

Martha quickly reappeared, picked the weapons up, and handed them to Hunter.

"You'll pay for this," Melvick said through clenched teeth.

"We'll see." I pointed them to the chairs, telling them to sit down.

I then saw a knife disappear from behind them. I knew that Linda had picked it up and hidden it on her person.

"Now." Commander Aggo 1 stepped in front of his son, Chancellor Aggo 2, and Melvick. "Who are you working for and why are you planning to take over our world?"

"We are not going to take over your world," Director Stener started to say as Melvick glared at him and said "Shut up idiot!"

"Take Melvick out of here," Commander Aggo 1 said to two of his men. "And keep a close watch on him," He said as they led him out of the room.

"Dad, what makes you think they are going to take over our world?" asked his son, looking at him.

"Answer me," the commander said, glaring at Stener and then at his son.

Stener gulped as Hunter grabbed him by the shoulder, picked

him up, then slammed him back into the chair—hard, almost knocking him to the ground. He gulped again and in an uneasy voice said, "We came from another galaxy, after picking up your radio transmissions. We have been observing you ever since you started moving out into the stars and thought we could work our way into your government slowly, taking over without having to invade you. You see, our home world's sun was dying and we do not have the resources or the manpower to take you over by force anymore."

As he sat there, I saw in his eyes that he was telling us the truth, but suspected there was more he was not yet saying. Looking at Commander Aggo 1, I said. "He is probably telling the truth but not all of it."

Glancing at Hunter, the commander inclined his head toward the director and nodded.

As Hunter started to reach for him again, Stener yelled, "No! No!" He then turned his head away and dropped his chin down. As Hunter stopped, Stener looked up and said, "When we got control of the government we were to send out a message and the rest of our people would come, bringing all of our military and civilians. They would say they were running from an enemy that had invaded our world and offer to stand with you against your enemy if you would give us a place to live. Then we would slowly take over your world and make it into our own."

"Why not find another world that was not populated to live on?" I asked. "There has to other worlds out there that would support life."

"Yes there are many, but they don't have the technology that you do and we don't have the people or the desire to live on a lower, underdeveloped world. We have lost so much technology we wouldn't know how to live without it." He said finally, looking sheepishly at us.

"If you had come to us, we would have helped you," said Chancellor Aggo 2 looking at him.

"Would you have? Or would you have thought we were lying and turned us away or even fought us?" Stener asked, looking at the chancellor.

"Um. . .yes," stammered Aggo 2. "I see what you mean.

CHAPTER 21

Suddenly we heard a loud scream echoing through the halls coming from the room where they had taken Melvick.

"You bastards, get me a f . . . doctor! I'm bleeding. I demand to see a doctor. I know my rights!"

"If you will quit moving around, I will get that wound dressed and see about getting you a doctor," was the response. "Now be quite." Which was followed immediately by another loud scream and more swearing. "There. That should hold you until a doctor can see you."

"Take him into the other room so they can question him. And keep Director Stener separate from the other prisoners," Commander Aggo 1 said to the man standing next to him.

As Director Stener was being led out of the door, Melvick was being brought out of the other room. Upon seeing Stener being led away, Melvick yelled loudly, "Don't tell them anything."

"Quiet, get in there." The guard gave him a slight shove.

"Do not push," Melvick stumbled and looked back over his shoulder at the man as he shuffled into the room.

"Sit down," Hunter said, pushing him so he sat down hard, landing in the chair Stener had just vacated. He let out a loud groan.

"Now," said Commander Aggo1. "What were you planning to do with Hunter and these women?"

"My arm is still bleeding," said Melvick crossly.

I looked at him and said, "The pain will quit before long. You know it could be worse. Now answer the question."

Just as I had said this the door was thrown open and ten armed men pushed their way into the room, not leaving us room to even turn around let alone defend ourselves. They shoved us roughly against the wall.

Linda disappeared again before they saw her.

As the lieutenant in charge of the squad was untying Melvick, he looked around and asked, "Is this all of them, sir?"

"Did you get the other ones?" Melvick asked.

"Yes sir, we have them under guard in the main conference room, sir. We are using it for a prison for now."

"Then I think we have them all," he said as he looked at us. "Wait . . . Where is that bitch you say is your wife Reaol 10? Linda . . . is that the name she is using now?"

"My daughter is not a bitch," said Mrs. Chan 2 stepping forward and slapping Melvick hard. A guard stepped in front of her, placing his hands and weapon on her chest, forcing her back.

Hunter, placing his hands on Martha's shoulders to comfort her said quietly, "It will be alright."

She nodded and slowly stepped back against the wall with the rest of us. "She's not a bitch," Martha said to Hunter, looking pleadingly at him.

"I know she's not. It will be alright." He put his arms around her and held her tight.

"Place them with the others and keep a close watch on them, especially them." He pointed to Hunter and me. "Don't let them talk," Melvick said as he leered at Abbrelle.

"Her," he said, pointing to Abbrelle. "Tie her in that chair. Get the rest of them out of here," He said impatiently. "Take them away." He repeated again.

"Yes sir." The lieutenant grabbed Abbrelle roughly by the arm and dragged her over to the chair, forcing her to sit. He pulled her arms roughly behind her back, causing her chest to thrust out, and started tying them.

"No!" I leaped at the guard, only to be struck a blow to the side of my head by one of the guards.

"I'll question her myself," said Melvick with a leer on his lips. "Get them out of here."

"You . . . stay here," he said to the lieutenant just as he was turning for the door.

"Sergeant," he said to the man who had stopped just out of the door. "Take them to the conference room with the rest of the prisoners and don't let any of them speak to one another."

"Yes sir." He saluted and turned around, heading us toward the makeshift prison.

"Close the door. No! On second thought, leave it open. I want them to hear what I am doing to her—her screams especially," he said half smiling, still leering at Abbrelle. He walked over to her and struck sharp blow across the face.

"Sir . . . is that wise?" asked the lieutenant in surprise.

He sharply said with a sneer on his lips, "They will expect a few marks on her. Most of the marks I leave will not show." He struck a hard blow to the center of her chest with an open hand, knocking her and the chair onto the floor. "Sit her up," he said to the lieutenant. "Don't be careful about how you do it, either," he said as the lieutenant was carefully trying to sit her up. The lieutenant grabbed the chair, forcing her breasts into his chest, and sat her up, blushing as he did so.

"Now," Melvick said, glaring at Abbrelle. "What were you going to do here?"

She looked up at him and spat in his face.

He slowly wiped the spittle off and slapped her across the face again, knocking her half out of the chair.

Once she was sitting back up again, she spat blood at him since she now had a cut on her lip, hitting him again on the face. The spit and blood on his face dripped down and off his chin.

Smiling, he wiped it off his face he struck her with a closed fist—hard—just below the right breast, knocking all the breath out of her and causing her to gasp for breath.

"Sir," the lieutenant said sharply.

"Quiet. The only reason you're here is to keep her in that chair and verify anything she says. Nothing else. You are not to comment on how I get the answers. Do I make myself clear!"

Yes . . . sir," the lieutenant stammered as he backed away.

"Now my dear, are you ready to tell me why you are here, or would you like some special . . . attention?"

Abbrelle looked him in the eyes and spat on him again. "Do your best."

He struck her hard to the chest again, knocking the chair backwards, and knocking Abbrelle completely out of the chair.

As she lay there gasping for breath, Melvick came and grabbed her by the shorts she was wearing, ripping them down her legs and off. "I hear you like to fight without these on," he said as he held them up for her to see. "Well there you are. Now get up and fight, if you can." He threw the shorts her. He then stood back, laughing and leering at her—as she struggled to stand up.

As she struggled to her feet, Melvick drew back his good leg to kick her, but fell hard to the floor as his other leg was suddenly knocked from under him. "Wha. . ." he started to say when a heavy object struck his head, knocking him unconscious.

The lieutenant stood there with his mouth open, as Abbrelle jumped up and rammed her head and shoulder into his chest, knocking all his breath from him. He started to fall and reached out with his hands trying to grab something on her so as to take her down with him. As his hands slid over her nude body, he found nothing to hold on to. He fell heavily to the floor, gasping for breath. When he looked up, he saw the heavy book coming down on his head. He threw an arm up and deflected the book as it descended toward him.

"Stop." he gasped. "I'll help you," he croaked before the book could hit him again. He lay there staring at the book seemingly floating in air by its self.

Abbrelle, after putting her shorts back on, realized that they would not stay on because of the rips they endured. She let them fall to the floor just as Linda popped into view and said, looking at Abbrelle, "Well, it looks like when you fight now, their attention will not be on your hand, anyway."

"No . . . " said the Lieutenant, now looking up at them both. "Quick. Scream!" he said to Abbrelle, a concerned look on his face. Gesturing with his hands he said again, "Scream." He then struck his hands together.

As understanding dawned on Abbrelle's face, she let out a blood-chilling scream, and then followed it with another softer scream, and followed that up with some softer moans.

"Sir. I think she is unconscious," he said as he quickly held a finger to his lips. He got gingerly to his feet and crossed to the door as two soldiers started up the hall toward the room. Stepping into the hall, he said in a firm, commanding voice, "Everything is under control. Return to your stations." When he turned and returned into the room, he saw Abbrelle had his weapon pointed at him.

"We had better tie him up and gag him," He pointed to Melvick.

After they had bound and gagged Melvick, Abbrelle, still pointing the weapon at the young lieutenant said, "Explain!"

"I was on guard duty," he said, trying not to look at her. "I saw you coming through the trees and instantly realized what was happening. I had just seen Melvick, with who he said were prisoners, drive in. When I saw the squad following you in the building, I kind of figured you may need some help. Oh, I'm Lieutenant Aggo 3, the Chancellor's son.

Commander Aggo 1 is my grandfather. Is the commander here?"

"Yes, David. I'm right behind you," said a firm but gentle voice.

"Grandfather!" he exclaimed as he turned around only to see Commander Aggo 1, his grandfather, holding a weapon on him.

"Grandfather?" he asked questioningly, looking at Aggo 1.

"He helped us," Abbrelle quickly said and went on to explain what had happened.

As I came running into the room, I slid to a stop and stood looking at them. But I looked mostly at Abbrelle standing there with bruises on most of her upper body—bruises which were starting to turn brilliant black and blue. Seeing her standing nude I ran over and hugged her tight. She let out a low moan, and I stepped away from her saying, "Sorry, I was just glad to see you are alright." I crossed to a locker on the far wall, opened it, took out a white lab coat, and handed it to her. "Put this on."

"How did you know . . . " she started to say, then closing her mouth, she just smiled. She nodded her head and said, "I know. You'll tell me later."

"Thank you for the help in the other room, Linda." I said, looking at her. "You should put some clothing on."

She just nodded in acknowledgement and "glimmered" some shorts on.

As Abbrelle was pulling the lab coat on, Christy and the rest of the men came running into the room. Most were forced to stay in the hallway since there was not enough room.

"We have them all secure sir," said a young lieutenant, saluting.

Christy, seeing Abbrelle looking like she had been in a terrible fight, ran over to her sister and took her by the shoulders. Trying to be careful and to not hurt her, she asked, "Are you OK?"

"I'm fine. A little sore, but fine. Thanks to Linda. If it wasn't for her I would probably be dead by now." She looked at Linda as Hunter pulled Abbrelle tightly into his arms. He reluctantly released her as Martha came into the room, running over to her daughter, grabbing her, and holding her tight.

"I was so scared when you did not reappear. What happened?"

As we were going over what each of us had done, a large squad of men came to the door followed by Chancellor Aggo 2.

Lieutenant David Aggo 3 said with authority, "Arrest him," pointing to Melvick, now sitting in the chair.

I MEET Abbrelle

After they took Melvick out, Chancellor Aggo 2 said to Commander Aggo 1, "May I speak to you?" He gestured for him to follow him into the hallway.

One week later, after everything had been sorted out, and some very damning evidence had been found, Commander Aggo 1 came to me. "I hear you are thinking of going back to your world."

"Yes, I have been. There are certain things I have to take care of there. I've been gone a long time. There are people I have to see and things I have to take care of. There are people that will wonder where I have been. But I would like to come back if I may." I looked at him hopefully.

"I see," Walt said, looking at me. "You know you will be missed here too, mostly by a certain person."

"Yes, I have been thinking about her too." I replied.

"Well, when you are ready to leave, let me know. I will have a ship ready to take you home."

Two weeks later, I went aboard the ship for my trip home. My new bride, Abbrelle Emulate-Stevenson walked up the ramp by my side, smiling happily.

EPILOGUE

One year later, I was sitting in our front room at my desk, looking out the window, trying to figure out how we would be able to return to Home Pride. I finally got all of my affairs settled and arranged it so we wouldn't have to spend all of our time here on Earth.

All of a sudden, there was a constant pealing ring of the front door bell—again.

Not again. It can't be, I thought. Smiling and hoping—the grin on my face getting larger.

"Dear, will you please get that before it wakes the baby?" Abbrelle called as she hurried into Dawn's room. "Who could it be? Ringing the bell like that? They should know better." She said angrily as she hurriedly went into the baby's room just as she started to cry.

"No, it can't be," I said again, still smiling hopefully as I got out of the chair—hoping I was right as I hurried to the door.

When I opened it, I was suddenly greeted by Christy jumping into my arms, hugging me tightly, and yelling surprise.

Staggering under her sudden, but light weight, I hugged her back as tightly as she was hugging me.

"Christy. . .how. . .when?" I stammered.

"May we come in, or are you just going to leave us standing out here?" Hunter said happily as he started pushing his way past me through the door.

"Darling who is it?" asked Abbrelle as she came out of little Dawn's room, holding her to her bare breast, letting her suckle. "I think she is going back to sleep," she said, still looking down at her. When she looked back up, she screamed, causing little Abbrelle to start crying loudly again.

"Christy! . . . Hunter! . . . Linda! . . .Commander!. . .sir. How . . . Wh . . .Why . . .Wha . . .What . . .When," she stammered as she looked up to see them all standing in the hall. She started running as fast as she cold with the baby still clutched in her arms to greet them.

"I came to see if you were ready to come back to work. But I can see you're not," said Walt Aggo 1, standing with a huge smile on his face. He come toward her and said, "Let me hold her." As she was still holding Abbrelle to her bare breast, the baby started crying as she was forced to release the nipple in her mouth.

As they all let the "glimmer" of clothing drop, I said, "Please come into the front room and have a seat." I gestured toward the front room.

Abbrelle said in a low voice, "No sir, not yet I'm not," looking lovingly down at little Abby." As Walt held her, tickling her under the chin and smiling down at her, Abbrelle said, "Excuse me, I have to go and change her." She took her from him and hurried back into the baby's room.

When Abbrelle returned from changing little Dawn, she started introducing her to everyone. Dawn cooed and babbled at them. She in turn was getting the usual Ooos and Ahhhs from everyone. They all gathered around her, trying to get a good look at her.

Looking up, she suddenly noticed little Elisabeth in Linda's arms. Linda had stepped away from the group holding her daughter in front of her breast to see better, and then sat down on the couch placing little Elisabeth on her lap.

"Oh, my," said Abbrelle. "She is beautiful. How old is she? Isn't she just darling?"

"Four months," replied Linda, handing her to Abbrelle.

"Let me hold her," she said as she was handing Dawn to Linda. They giggled together for causing the babies to collide with each other when they tried to hand them to each other. Then they sat there, talking about the little ones as they both looked adoringly at them.

The door bell rang again, normally, this time.

"See, I told you that you weren't to just hold it in," Hunter said to Christy, but smiling at her as he said it.

Both Christy and I broke out into laughter at the remark, thinking of the first time we had met.

"What is so funny?" Hunter asked, looking at us both questioningly.

We looked at each again other and started laughing harder.

"I'll tell you later," Christy said, still laughing and waving her hand at Hunter as I got up to answer the door.

"Lorene! Please come in. I have some people I want you to meet." I led her into the front room where she stopped and stared open-mouthed at the people sitting there—seeing them all sitting there, for us on Earth, only half dressed. She gasped and then broke into a huge smile as realization dawned on her, her face lighting up.

"This is Abbrelle's sister, Christy," I said as I started introducing them. "Her brother, Hunter, and his wife, Linda, with their darling daughter, Elisabeth. Did you ever get that mess with your marriage license straightened out?" I asked, looking at Hunter.

"Not yet. Does it matter?" answered Linda, smiling.

"No." I smiled back at her. "You know some of us can see through 'glimmer.'"

She just smiled and spread her . . . a little.

"And this is Commander Walt Aggo 1," I said. I finished up the introductions, gesturing to each of them as I said their names. They all smiled back at the introduction. Then I turned, smiling at Lorene when I had finished introducing them, and introduced her.

"But . . . I . . . They're not?. . .Are they? I didn't believe you." She stammered, looking at me and then back at them. "I thought it was just a fictional story like all the rest of the stories you have written.

Abbrelle sat down next to Christy, who was now holding her niece and said, "Oh, I think we will be gone for a while," Abbrelle said happily to me, then at Lorene as she looked back at her, standing with her mouth open.